MAGNUS

George Mackay Brown (1921–96) was one of the twentieth century's most distinguished and original writers. His lifelong inspiration and birthplace, Stromness in Orkney, moulded his view of the world, though he studied in Edinburgh, and later under Edwin Muir at Newbattle Abbey College. In 1941 he began his battle with tuberculosis and lived an increasingly reclusive life in Stromness, but he produced, in spite of his poor health, a regular stream of publications from 1954 onwards. These included *Loaves and Fishes* (1959), collections of short stories, *A Calendar of Love* (1967), *A Time to Keep* (1969) and *Hawkfall* (1974), *Greenvoe* (1972), *Time in a Red Coat* (1984) and a steady output of prose and poetry, notably the novel *Beside the Ocean of Time* (1994) which was shortlisted for the Booker Prize and winner of the Saltire Book of the Year. His work is permeated by the layers of history in Scotland's past, by quirks of human nature and religious belief and by a fascination with the world beyond the horizons of the known.

He was honoured by the Open University and by Dundee and Glasgow Universities. The enduringly successful St Magnus Festival of poetry, prose, music and drama, held annually in Orkney, keeps his memory alive and is his lasting memorial.

GEORGE MACKAY BROWN

Magnus

Polygon

First published in 1973 by Hogarth Press.
This edition published in 2008 by Polygon,
an imprint of Birlinn Limited

West Newington House
10 Newington Road
Edinburgh
EH9 1QS

9 8 7 6 5 4 3 2 1

www.birlinn.co.uk

ISBN 978 1 84697 062 7

British Library Cataloguing-in-Publication Data
A catalogue record for this book is available from the British Library

Typeset by Hewer Text UK Ltd, Edinburgh
Printed and bound by Clays Ltd, St Ives plc

Contents

Readers of *An Orkney Tapestry* may notice that the two old tinkers of the 'Martyr' chapter appear, more full-fleshed, in this novel. Those who saw, in Orkney in August 1972, the play *The Loom of Light*, written for the St Magnus Cathedral Restoration Fund, may also notice certain resemblances.

G.M.B.

The Plough

One spring morning all the peasants of Birsay were out on the bishop's land, ploughing behind their oxen.

The land went in a gradual fertile sweep from the hill Revay to the shore of Birsay. Just off the shore was a steep green island, with a church on it, and a little monastery, and a Hall. A sleeve of sea shone between the ploughlands and The Brough of Birsay (as this island was called). Occasionally the peasants could hear the murmur of plainsong from the red cloister.

The wild geese flew over.

The peasants put their slow patient scars on the fields.

A young man and woman crossed the heather to a new strip of tilth on the lower slope of Revay Hill. The woman was solid and squat and redfaced; she carried a wooden plough over her shoulder. The man yawned as he went. One or two of the peasants called out to him that he was sleeping late in the morning nowadays. He laughed back at them – a flash of teeth, a gust of lewd confident laughter. One peasant shouted, 'It's as bad as that, is it, Mans? You even have to take Hild to the field with you.' The young man laughed again, but Hild his wife hung her head and blushed. 'No,' said Mans, 'the ox is lame. Damn you, Sven, I'm not as randy as that. Hild will have to pull the plough this morning, that's all that's for it.'

They reached the end of their rig. This small field had been broken open with mattocks two years before and it was good fruitful earth, but the undersoil kept thrusting up primeval stones and roots to the sun, and it was still difficult to plough.

Mans fitted the yoke on the thick shoulders of his wife. 'I'm sorry, woman,' he said. 'With luck we'll be finished before sunset. The ox will maybe be better tomorrow.'

'We'll manage,' said Hild. 'I'm as strong as any ox.'

'*Plough out that new strip on the side of Revay,* he says to me,' said Mans, mocking the officiousness of Arn the factor. '*Plough it out tomorrow morning. My intention is that barley should be sown in it this year.* Says I, *The ox is lame, he stumbled on a stone.* Says he, *You've got a new strong wife, haven't you? Yoke her. What's a stone or two, neither here nor there,* says he. The bastard.'

Now the plough was set, between Hild and Mans, like a great key to open the winter field to the sun and full bounty of harvest. Mans prodded his wife with a stick. 'Get up,' he said. 'Go slow and straight. Don't lurch.' Hild moved forward, dragging the plough. Once or twice she jerked to a halt. Then Mans dropped the shafts and picked up a stone from in front of the share and threw it aside. 'Get up,' he shouted. The sun rose higher. They finished the first of the seven furrows. Hild drew her forearm across her shining brow. 'Turn round,' said Mans. 'We're not stopping. We must get the whole rig ploughed before the sun goes down.'

The plough went, waveringly, making a second scratch across the flank of the hill, borne by the woman, driven by the man. They were bowed under the immensity of their labour. They seemed to bear the sun on their shoulders. At the end of the second furrow – a lucky one, because there were no stones, only the sigh and suck of steadily broken clay – they saw that the other peasants had stopped working. They were sitting here and there about the hill eating their bread and cheese. 'We're not stopping yet,' said Mans. 'We lay in bed too long this morning. We'll stop and eat when we've finished the next furrow.'

They turned again. They had hardly taken three ponderous steps when Hild cried out and clapped her hands to her shoulder. 'What's wrong now?' said Mans, shaking the stilts of the plough.

'Another stone, I think,' said Hild.

Mans came round and dragged a huge stone from the side of the share. He lifted it and went reeling to the edge of the rig and dropped it. 'There's enough stones in this field to build a barn,' he said when he came back. 'Only if I did that, the bishop would put up the rent for sure. *Another stone of butter, I think,* Arn the factor would say. *Yes, another stone of butter, and a stone of cheese, and I think perhaps an extra day's labour in his lordship's field at harvest, my man* . . . Bloody parasites.'

At the end of the third furrow Mans unyoked Hild. They sat down in the heather. Hild took two wedges of white cheese and a bannock out of her basket. She broke the bannock in two and gave the larger piece, and a wedge of cheese, to Mans. Hild made a sign of the cross over the food. 'Bless all Thy gifts to us from Thy bounty. Amen.' Mans was already eating. 'Say Amen,' said Hild. Mans mumbled something through a mouthful of cheese and bread; a runnel of grey juice ran into his beard.

Something was happening over on The Brough. That tranquil island was suddenly like a disturbed beehive. A servant woman walked among an outflurry of hens and stooped and went back into the kitchen of the Hall with six twitching corpses. The bell for Terce was late, and was succeeded almost at once by the bell for Sext. Long white coats, bald heads, hurried here and there through the cloister. A man with a knife dragged a pig, thinly squealing, towards the dunghill in the yard. Once the young bishop himself appeared bareheaded, and looked over towards the Hall, and went back into the church. There were important guests at the earl's Hall that day. They moved about in their stylish clothes in the sunlight, bright as bees and butterflies. One came down to the water's edge and dipped his fingers in a pool. A young couple, hand in hand, climbed towards the summit of the island, where it was suddenly shorn off into a line of tall red Atlantic-facing cliffs. The kitchen began to reverberate with the noise of pots and pans. The island had a larger skirt now, for the tide had been ebbing all morning and leaving swathes of seaweed and un-covered rocks. Soon it would be an island no more, and the few peasant women who were standing in a knot on the Birsay shore would be able to walk across to The Brough, if they got official permission.

'What's going on?' said Mans, sucking the last of the juice out of his red curly moustache.

'Surely you haven't forgotten,' said Hild. 'Today's the wed-ding. The lord Erlend and the lady Thora. Everybody in Orkney knows that.'

'If they don't know now,' said Mans, 'they will know it next winter. They'll know it all right when their taxes go up. To keep the wine in their cups and the silk on their backs. The blood-suckers.'

'You mustn't speak like that,' said Hild. 'I saw the lady Thora on her horse yesterday. She's a bonny girl, right enough. She smiled at me, riding down between the fields. I wish I could see her in her bridal gown. I hope the wedding won't take place till evening, then I might have a chance of seeing her, like the women down at the shore there.'

'If I was you,' said Mans, 'I would save my breath to pull the plough.' He got to his feet. Hild followed him. He lifted the yoke. She bowed her shoulders to receive it. He angled the plough at the earth.

The fourth furrow was heavy going. The share struck on gray stones and red stones. Mans threw them aside. Once the plough got wedged between two stones, and when Mans pulled them up he saw a well of darkness underneath – not the rich earth darkness but the uncanny hollow darkness of a troll's house. He peered inside, and saw an underground chamber of large crude stones. These trolls' houses were common in this part of

Orkney. If you were brave enough to explore deeper you might find a few human skeletons, with cairngorms and pearls and silver brooches. But only a few of the young Vikings had the courage to go after such terrible treasure. Mans did not throw these stones aside. He replaced them carefully over the hole and covered it up with earth. He beat the earth flat with his feet. Hild turned round and crossed herself three times. 'Get up,' said Mans. The plough stoddered forward, round the breached cellar.

Down at the shore now, there were a score of women waiting.

Between the fifth and the sixth furrows two young tinkers, a man and a girl, crossed the shoulder of the hill. The man was carrying a dead rabbit. They hesitated at the edge of the rig, then the girl began to walk among the furrows. She stood for a moment in the third furrow, looking uncertainly from the man tinker to the two peasants. The plough shivered to a halt.

'Get back off the ploughed land,' shouted Mans. 'Where the hell do you think you're going? Off with you.'

The tinker girl skipped back to her mate. She was a dark lithe creature. Varying fires – rage, mockery, scorn – burned in her eyes. Her face smouldered at Mans and Hild. She had large flashing eyes; as if they drew their light direct from the clear well of the sun.

Her man said, humbly and gently, 'I'm sorry, sir. We're making for the shore, to cook our supper. It's shorter this way. I sprained my ankle up on the hill.'

'It's not as if the seed was in,' said the girl. 'I wasn't doing any harm.'

'Cross a ploughed field once more this summer,' said Mans slowly and darkly, 'just let me hear of you putting one foot in anybody's corn, and the factor will know about it. The factor hanged three tinkers in Caithness last winter.'

The tinker girl put a black glower on Mans. Her man took her by the elbow, anxiously, in case she said any more. They veered

away, going round by the side of the field. Before they turned
their faces to the shore, the girl jumped once in and out of a
furrow. The girl yelled in derision. She squeezed up her face and
stuck out her tongue. Hild looked round, terrified, at the
hideous gargoyle (for tinkers, with priests and witches, can
put a curse on simple people). Then the girl went leaping down
the hill, and her man followed hirpling a long distance behind.
Her mockery faded among the rocks and sand dunes.

'Bloody scum,' said Mans.

'No, but you must be careful what you say to the likes of
them.'

They paused at the end of the sixth furrow.

Bells, thin and purified with distance, began to peal from the
steeple of the church in the island (that was now an island no
more, for the last thread of sea had snapped, and the women of
Birsay had begun to troop over, picking their way carefully with
raised skirts among the seaweed and the rockpools). On the
hither shore only the two tinkers were left. They stooped,
gathering bits of driftwood from the ebb. Up and down and
round the bells swung, they nodded, they brimmed with joyous
sound, the bronze tongues struck the bronze palates, and all
these mouths trembled, now one, now another, high and low,
all different, but making a single splendour of sound, an
epithalamion.

The figures that erupted suddenly about the open door of the
Hall were no bigger than bees, from where Mans and Hild stood
among their furrows. These were the wedding guests – the
gentry and large farmers and important merchants of Orkney
and Caithness. A lonely mitred figure appeared at the door of
the church. The swarm of wedding guests unfolded to reveal
two figures, one in white, one in scarlet. The pair moved slowly
towards the church door. The wedding guests seethed after
them. All moved in a trance of happy sound. The air was rich.
The bishop raised his right hand. Bridegroom and bride bowed.

They touched his offered jewelled hand with their mouths. They passed first into the church. The bells trembled and fell silent, one after the other. After that bronze exultation, the fragile choir voices. *Homo quidam fecit cenam magnam,* sang the monks inside. The bishop followed bridegroom and bride into the web of sacred song. The wedding guests, two by two, stooped under the arch.

'We have one more furrow to do,' said Mans.

Breaking the last furrow, they were very tired. Hild stumbled once or twice. When the plough struck a stone she felt as though her shoulder had been wrenched from its socket. She groaned. Mans, stumbling after the plough, began to mutter and curse to himself about this and that. '*Your wife,* says he, *she'll do till the ox gets better. Yoke her . . .*' And on he went, mumbling occasionally 'scum', 'parasites', 'bastards', 'bloodsuckers', though whether he meant the factor or the bridal pair or the tinkers at their fire on the shore or the stony furrow Hild did not know. Once or twice Mans spat in disgust. Hild's back ached as though she had lain a winter on a bed of boulders. She saw that her feet were plodding through scree and tufts of heather. 'Woa!' cried Mans. 'We're finished, thank God. Where do you think you're going?'

They stretched themselves for a while in the heather. All the other peasants had gone home with their ploughs and oxen.

The ocean tilted up, slowly, to meet the sun. In Christ Church the nuptial Mass was being celebrated, though of course nothing of the ceremony could be heard from the sunset flank of Revay; nothing, except one small exquisite tinkle through the stillness of the sea and the seabirds. 'The Lord Christ is in the church now,' whispered Hild. She sat up. She saw the Birsay women kneeling round the church door.

Mans muttered among the heather.

'It's time we were going home,' said Hild at last.

The sun was a bleeding wound along the horizon.

Evening brought a great silence, in which there were only small sounds – the lap of a wave, the thud of a rabbit or a hare, the pleep-pleep of a seabird.

Mans put the plough over his shoulder. He was too tired to say yes or no.

Half-way down to their croft, Hild looked back. There was a yellow-and-red flicker outside the cave; that would be the tinkers stewing their rabbit.

'For Christ's sake hurry up,' said Mans. 'I'm hungry.'

It grew darker. The church was possessed by a still measured murmur. It came, a thread of blessing, over the sea. Hild paused to listen.

Suddenly Mans was furiously angry. He stood on the peat road and raged. 'The blessing,' he shouted. 'What kind of blessing do they need, other than what they've got!'. . . Hild walked on. She felt sad and a bit frightened when Mans was in this mood. They were poor humble folk – they always would be – God had ordained it so – it was foolish, not to say impious, to complain the way Mans did whenever there was a bit of extra labour to do on the land.

She walked on, alone. There was a different sound from the sea now. The tide had turned. The gray flood was beginning to pour in from the west. Slowly the waters encroached on the wide shore that led from the ploughlands to The Brough. The darkening sea was full of echoes and boomings and sonorities.

When Hild looked round again Mans had disappeared. She knew where he had gone. Prem the weaver's door further up the hill stood open and she could see a few men sitting round the lamp and the barrel. Prem, who was a bachelor, kept a kind of ale-house in addition to his loom and his hundred sheep. 'No wife,' thought Hild, 'would allow that kind of carry-on in her house.' . . . Like most of the women, she disliked drink and the changes it wrought in her man. A few peasants and fishermen gathered in Prem's cottage in the evening. Hild hated it when

Mans went there, for it was hard to say in what shape he would come home. He was one of the kind that wouldn't stop drinking till the barrel was empty. When he got drunk he was generally violent and satirical.

Hild was too tired to eat anything in her cold cottage. She knelt beside the bed and said *Our Father, Hail Mary, Glory Be.* Then, because her whole body ached, she lay down on the straw and sacking. She prayed to God that Mans would come home from the ale-house sober. She prayed that the lord Erlend Thorfinnson and the lady Thora would have many happy years together, and children growing about them, and children's children to sweeten their age. She prayed that the field they had ploughed would yield enough for them to eat next winter. She prayed that there would be no more war in the islands in their time: she thought with horror of the burning houses, the young men with the savage frightened mouths, the women going among the wounds and corpses at the shore, the ships that sailed into the west and never returned. *Give peace in our time, Lord*, she whispered in the darkness. She wondered briefly why, when all the other women in Birsay seemed to bear a new infant regularly each winter since their marriage, her own womb was still untroubled. Could it be that she was barren? *Fruit of the womb of the blessed Mary*, she prayed, *give me a child in this house, to sing to in a crib in the corner.* She prayed once more that Mans would not get drunk, and in the middle of that prayer she fell asleep.

She awoke to the gnawing in her shoulders, to the gray half-light before dawn, to the bitter taste of unanswered prayer. For Mans was very drunk. He was drunk in the worst way, swaying and shouting and cursing in the open door. He wanted food. He had had a hard day's work and he was hungry. Why was the fire out? The house was cold. He had had no supper. This was a poor welcome for a hardworking man to get. There should be bread and ale on the table. What kind of a slut had he married at all?

Hild got out of bed without saying a word. She stirred the gray embers and at once there was a hearth-flame. She broke a peat and added it to the fire. She lit the candle from the flame and set it in the stone water-niche in the wall. She took bread and cheese and milk from the cupboard and put them on the table. She kissed the loud ale-reeking mouth. 'Sit down and eat now,' she said.

But Mans would not sit down. He would not eat. He had said a lot of dangerous things in the ale-house and what he had said might be reported, for the world was full of tale-tellers and arse-kissers, but he didn't care, it was the truth, and he would say it again and again. 'This is the way I see it, Hild,' he said. 'The work of the world is done by poor peasants. Now listen. This is the way it is. It's common sense. The honest labourers, they're kept under by a few parasites. Yes, parasites. What parasites? It stands to reason. Leave that fire alone and listen. A parasite is a person who does no work, no, but he lives in luxury all the same. And who provides the parasite with his silks, and his silver and his flagons? *I* do,' said Mans, and struck the table with his fist, so that the candle flame shook and some of the milk splashed over on to the floor. 'Sven does. Prem does. All the poor people of Orkney do.'

'Keep your voice down,' said Hild.

'The names of the parasites should be beat round the parish with a bell,' said Mans. 'The earl. The bishop. The factor. The landowners.'

'The bishop is a good man,' said Hild.

'He's a parasite,' said Mans. 'A parasite and a hypocrite.' He twisted his face into a passable mask of Gulielmus Orcad and clasped his hands and gave his head an ecclesiastical tilt. '*I join you now in holy wedlock*,' he intoned. '*Lord Erlend and Lady Thora. May Mans that poor peasant keep you in plenty all the days of your life. May he sweat out his guts for you every day, till he drops dead in the furrows. And when the two earls fall afighting, a*

*thing they do from time to time, may there always be folk like
Mans to stand in front of your lordship and your ladyship and take
the swords in his guts.'* . . . He raised his hand in mock blessing.

'You're a good mimic,' said Hild wearily. 'But tell me in the
morning.'

Mans sat down on the stool beside the fire. He looked at the
blood and blisters on his hands.

'I am your man and I love you,' he said in a thick tired voice.
'Come to bed.'

'Yes,' said Hild, 'come to bed.'

She unloosed the thongs at his throat and waist and feet.

'The worst parasite of all is the king of Norway,' said Mans
darkly. He lay down and feel asleep at once; and Hild knew that
that night another of her prayers would not be answered. But
she was glad that he was safely home, with peace on his mouth
at last.

She went to close the door.

The guest-chamber of the Hall was lighted up. The sea lapped
high against the cliffs of the island. There would be drinking and
music and laughter there till the sun got up.

The young man in the Hall of Birsay, the bridegroom, suddenly
leaves the feast; or rather he is lured away from the revelry by a
group of colluding friends whose behaviour all evening towards
him has been a mixture of mockery and courtesy. Having recently
deserted him, as if casually, to whisper together in a corner, they
come about the bridegroom now, these conspirators, in ones and
twos, where he is sitting nervous and alone at the high table with
his wine-cup. (The bride has been summoned away by her
women some time before, and that also has been a conspiracy
and a secret.) The young men come about the bridegroom
carrying a jug of new wine. He must taste it before any of them.
They make a few unseemly but appropriate jokes, about maiden-
heads, battering rams, enchanted caves, the black rose of

midnight, etc., and snigger, and one nudges him gently in the ribs, and then he too smiles, but wanly. He takes a sip of the hot spiced wine and sets the cup down again. 'More, Erlend,' says Thorkel Peterson his best friend, 'there's a long night in front of you.' 'Yes,' says the bridegroom's elder brother Paul, 'you must keep your strength up . . .' They all laugh again. There is a flutter of winks here and there about the table – open shameless winks; they are not concerned with the bridegroom's finer feelings any more.

Soon they have had enough of the tomfoolery. When the new flagons have been brought in by the women, and plates of honeyed bread, and the musicians have paused to take a little refreshment, and the older guests are melling about the chair of the old earl, Arnor the poet who is in the conspiracy also gives the signal – a harp-stroke, a single high burning pure ecstatic cleaving of the hubbub and the chatter. Then the young men take Erlend Thorfinnson by the arms and shoulders, they hoist him to his feet, gently but firmly they manhandle him out of the festive hall, they bundle him and urge him (and he all the while making a token show of resistance) into the corridor. The nupital chamber is a small room at the end of the corridor, in the west part of the Hall. They herd him along. One holds a candle. One goes ahead and opens the dark door. On the table beside the bed is a flagon of wine and two silver cups. There the young men leave Erlend. They bow themselves out, half mocking, half grave. They warn him not to show his face again before he has performed the dark deed of heroism which has been assigned to him and to him alone by the gods. Before he turns to go Thorkel Peterson jerks loose the thong of Erlend's shoe, and winks, as if to say, 'Now the ceremony is under way. I leave the rest of the disrobing to a more delicate hand.'

Thora the bride, in the chamber of the looms, has been clustered about with women for the past hour and more.

There are Anna and Solveig and Sara, the three young women
who make tapestries for the Hall and vestments and altar-
cloths for the church. Tana who milks the cows and makes
butter and cheese in the cold room next to the byres is
present, and also Teig who guts and smokes the fish; her
hands still smell of the sea although she has rubbed them
together most of the morning in the sweet water of the burn.
There is even Cinders who keeps the many fires going in the
Hall, and sweeps the ashes, and covers the embers at night.
The women of course would not behave like this normally to
the lady Thora; they always drop their eyes and murmur
whenever she passes them in the corridor. But tonight they
chatter familiarly all about her. The three mysteries of love
and death and birth knit all women into a sisterhood. In
addition these women are all a little flushed and tongue-loose
with wine. They have untied Thora's hair and drawn combs
through the long bright crackling tresses and cascades. They
have taken off her shoes and then her white linen dress, and
touched herbal water to her shoulders and feet. All this they
do laughing and lightly gossiping to one another, and Tana
repeats a small bridal rhyme, a rune of fertility, the meaning
of which is not at all clear but she has learned it from her
grandmother. In the middle of all this palaver Thora is the
only still one. Once she trembles a little, and Cinders the
humble keeper of fires cries out, 'Is she cold then, the poor
thing! She'll be warm enough before morning.' They all laugh,
except Thora. Cinders kicks the peats and a flame roars up out
of the heart of them, till the bride's nakedness is hung with
yellow veils like thinnest shivering silk from India or Byzantium. It is time now. They have heard, ten wavefalls ago, the
prearranged signal from the great hall – Arnor's harp-stroke.
The bridegroom has gone to his chamber. Still they are loth to
take their eyes and their hands from the lady, who stands
meek and helpless among them. Teig's fingers go among her

hair, gently, for the twentieth time. Solveig takes up a phial
and touches a little more oil-of-thyme to Thora's throat. And
Teig the fish girl (she will never have the opportunity again)
even goes so far as to kiss the cold shoulder. But now they
really must go. Anna the seamstress, who is the oldest woman
present, holds open the light white embroidered nightgown.
Solveig and Sara take Thora's arms and push them gently into
the wide sleeves. Anna fastens the linen rope about the waist.
All is ready now. The girls have stopped their twittering and
fluttering. Cinders lights the red candle at the fire and gives it
to Anna. They arrange themselves. They move, a silent
procession, with the still white figure in the centre, towards
the nuptial chamber. Anna holds the candle aloft; the corridor
is a web of moving shadows. Anna knocks lightly three times
at the door.

They wait, it seems, for a long time (but it must have been
only for as long as it takes a moth to pass through a flame).
Cinders and Teig begin to cry, one after the other – Cinders
gently, dabbing the back of her hand to her eyes; and Teig
sobbing and choking as though something terrible had happened – her pigeon had flown away perhaps, or Freya the
housekeeper had struck her for filleting the haddocks badly.

'Who is there?' says a low voice from inside. It is so low the
women have to stretch their necks to hear. It is hardly more
than broken breath.

Anna says at once, 'The lady Thora, the wife of Erlend
Thorfinnson, is at the door. We have brought the bride to
the bridegroom.'

'Open the door, let her come in,' says the voice (and the
women can hear how it trembles in the darkness).

They wait. They would very much like to see the inside of the
bridal chamber, especially the bed. They long to have a glimpse
of the bridegroom standing among the candles. How will he
receive the bride? He will have to kiss her, of course. Perhaps

with no more ado he will lift her in his arms and carry her to the bed and lay her down. Anna has known a bridegroom and bride to stand staring at each other in a white trance before the slowly closing door hid the rest of the story from her eyes.

This time they will not have the chance. They have seen and done enough for one night, for women and girls in their humble station. They have glutted themselves like moths round the ceremonial flame. Thora asserts herself for the first time that night. She whispers, 'Thank you, you may go now.' She raises her hand. She points back the way they have come. The women linger, turn, go. At the end of the corridor Anna looks back once. Thora waits till the last susurration of their feet has faded. Then she raises her hand to the latch . . .

From here on the voice of the story-teller must be still, or at best it can only say, *After the wedding, when the dance and the wine-cup were still going round, Thora was carried to Erlend's chamber, and they lay together, and she conceived that night.*

But to celebrate the mystery properly the story-teller must give way to a ritual voice.

Arnor the Earl's poet left the Hall at midnight. He was tired of the ranting and whine of the pipes. His second-best harp had been besieged all night by that brutish noise. He went away quietly while the musicians' flagon – filled every hour – went from mouth to mouth. The night air was cold and delicious on his brow. He walked to his little hut near the crag-edge. He lit his candle and set it on the stone shelf. He sat down on the edge of his bed and untied the thong of his shoe. He remembered the purse at his waist – a sudden bounty and windfall – the Jutland crown that Paul Thorfinnson had given him earlier that evening for performing a simple enough task: some sort of love signal, he was given to understand from the lewd wink that Paul Thorfinnson bestowed on him along with the heavy round of silver. All he had had to do – as soon as the steward brought the first supper flagon to the earl's table – was to pluck his harp loudly once. He had done it. He had sent a single pure passionate note welling from the heart of the instrument; he was proud of that vivid star of sound; it must have searched into every corner of the great building. All the wedding guests had been startled; Earl Thorfinn had frowned across at him, the wine-soaked cake half-way to his lips. Arnor went to the door now and opened it and peered here and there into the night. He came back inside and barred the door. He prised open a loose stone in the floor and took out an iron-bound box. He dropped the Jutland crown among a sklinter of other coins and listened happily to the rich ringing, then he closed the box and set it once more in its dark well and replaced the flagstone. The ranting of the pipes began again, muted and monotonous. He unthonged his other shoe, and yawned. He set his workaday harp in the corner. The eye of a mouse glittered at him; he stamped his foot; the jewel vanished among small scrapes and scurries. Another monotony, cold and thin-spun, came from the church – the monks at their matins. Now he did not feel like sleep. There were too many fumes of the mulled wine on his palate and in his nostrils – too much bad sound in his ears – and certain images were beginning to stir at the edge of his mind. He took down his ceremonial silver-and-ivory harp – Earl Thorfinn's gift – from the wall. He sat down once more on the bed. The candle dribbled and wavered. Before dawn Arnor Earlsskald composed Three Sacred Bridal Songs for the high-born pair who, even as he gave the strings a first delicate fingering, were laid together in love; and while a great sacrificial host surged between the loins of bridegroom and bride, and among them a particular chosen seed, a summoned one, the sole ultimate destined survivor of all that joyous holocaust.

THREE SACRED BRIDAL SONGS

I

There was music in the hall a while back
  Feet still rise and fall. The guests are
  still dancing. The musicians puff their
  cheeks, unfold their fingers.

There is a monotony of voices under the arch
  The monks are at their matins now.

There is music written all across the night
  The planets are making an utterance
  over the unuttered seed.

No, but all my body is struck and blown
through, it is possessed with hierarchies and
orders of very sweet sound
  That is the music of *pax borealis*: the
  king, the two earls, the bishop,
  landowners, merchants, priests,
  peasants, beggars, beasts, furrows,
  fish, stones.

Listen. I think the harp has a wound. The
strings are broken
  That music will be bound up.

Forget that. There is a song at the end of
the corridor
  Let her come. Let the bride come
  now to a white unbroken bed.

Magnus

II

The loom is set. What will you weave, lady?
A web for an earl. A storied coat, jet and
gules, the heavy folds of state. My son will
sit in the council. He will visit his people –
laird and peasant and tramp. He will
cross over to the embattled ship behind
the arrows.

*What will you weave in the long loom of
your body?*
A green coat. The boy will carry his hawk
to the hill. He will drink wine under the
leaves with other young men. He will stroke
a harp. He will move pieces of ivory over the
chessboard. He will cool his bright flesh in
a rockpool.

What will the bride tread out on the shuttle?
The old mouths have told me. I weave
nothing. Unknown fingers fix the threads
in me. The shuttles fly and cross in my
womb. From the fingers of Fate issue it may
be a red cloth, or a black cloth, or hodden,
or stuff of motley, or tissue of cloth-of-gold.

But what will you weave, Lady Thora?
Blow out the lamp now. There is a hand at
the latch. Now I pray to Christ and the
Blessed Immaculate Virgin and to all saints
and martyrs that this shape I imagine in
my body, this boy, may wear the white
coat of innocence always. War to redden it,
intrigue to fray it, lust to filthy it, treachery

to tear it: these things must be. But I pray
that his soul may never be wrapped in the
seamless flame of eternal loss. I pray that
he may bring his white weave continually,
this Magnus, to the waters of grace, and
in the hour of his death to the last
brightest rinsings of absolution.

Weave now, girl, with your five hallowed desires

III
What is the lost cry in the heart of the earth?
I am wounded. I have taken a wound in
my flesh. The lips of it will never come
together. Fire has been thrust deep in
the wound. My flesh is branded.

IT IS THE SUN. IT IS THE PLOUGH AND
THE SOWER.

A Boy and a Seal

Seven boys stood at the shore of Birsay. They had been arriving separately there all through the morning. They did not know each other; they would have liked to introduce themselves, but they were still too shy. One of them skidded flat stones over the shrinking surface of the sea. One walked back and fore on the seabanks above, occasionally turning his face inland towards the peasants working in the fields. One drew delicate patterns on the sand with the point of his shoe and rubbed them out again, time after time.

One or other of the boys looked occasionally towards the further island shore, where an elderly tonsured man was standing with a piece of writing in his hand. It was obvious that these seven boys and the monk had some kind of business with each other. As yet they could not communicate because a fringe of water separated Birsay from the island. It was ebbing, but it would be an hour and more before the meeting took place among the seaweed.

The sea withdrew with mournful plangent sounds.

It seemed in fact that two of the boys were acquainted. From time to time they met each other's eye, and then their mouths relaxed a little and they half raised their hands; but it seemed that they did not wish to break the ring of silence into which all seven of them were gathered; and always at last the dark boy would fall to studying with a serious face the washed pebbles at his feet.

The sea fell away from a large limpet-studded rock. The shells glittered with water and sun. The limpets stirred. The shells grew gray in the sun.

Once or twice the monk called across to the boys, but he was an elderly man and his words were scattered in the vastness.

The sea drew back. It left first one rockpool, then another. A tall straw-haired boy put his freckled hand into the newest rockpool, and cried softly with the sudden pain of it. The water was very cold. Winter had not yet gone out of it.

The boy with black tight curls and blue eyes had long since climbed down from the seabanks, but still he sometimes turned his back on the shrinking sea and looked at the inland fields. Most of the peasants were hidden from him now by folds in the hill; he could see only one peasant half a mile away sowing seed in his rig on the side of Revay, striding like a soldier and slashing seed into the furrows with both hands. The boy had asked that peasant an hour before the way to The Brough of Birsay. The man had put a remote look on him, as if he had interrupted some religious rite, and had merely grunted, bending and filling his seed basket from the sack at the end of the rig. At last a broad-set woman had come out of one of the huts and said kindly, 'There it is, down there, that steep island with the big buildings on it and the kirk. But the sea won't be out for an hour yet.' . . . Then she had turned and reproached the sower, 'You could have spoken to the boy, Mans.' . . . The man had not had a word for her either; he was half-way up the rig, striding like a man in a trance . . . The boy, looking back now from the dividing waters, saw that the churlish one was still at his rite. The sowing of the seed would go on all morning.

The channel dwindled. A new piece of sand was uncovered; it shone for a moment, then was a gray drab hump.

A rather small boy with a sensuous mouth and restless eyes and hands had heard something on the shore of the island. He stood with tilted head, listening. Was it only the suck and glut of the retreating waters? No, there it came again, a small sad cry. 'The seal hunters,' he said, and looked across at the tall red-headed boy that he knew slightly. Their eyes met; their mouths relaxed in a smile. Then the dark boy turned his face once more to the centre of pain.

The ebb was leaving swathes of red and brown seaweed behind it, dulse, bladderwort, tangles, and sea anemones, and small crabs that as yet liked the warm pools more than the cold immensities of the Atlantic.

One boy lingered well behind the others. He had not taken off his shoes on the dry sand before beginning to cross over and now the skins oozed water. The boy lingered and shivered, and his cheeks were blue with cold. 'You'd better hurry,' said the boy who had been watching for a while the seed-time on Revay. 'The tide comes in again, remember. You'll be wetter than ever when that happens.' The boy with the wet feet said nothing, and the one who had spoken saw with embarrassment that he was crying. His face streamed, tears fell among the cold shells.

Monotony mingled with monotony. The monks in the choir began to sing Terce. They imitated with their voices the time-lessness of heaven. Mildly they mocked, among the sounds of the ebb, the urgencies and ambitions of men.

One boy had a harp on his shoulder. He walked very circumspectly, careful where he placed his feet among the seaweed and the slippery stones. He stumbled once, and the strings cried out. The boy blushed, and halted for a moment. He advanced more slowly then against the almost-vanquished music of the sea.

For now the shore itself was like a half-shattered harp. Only a few strands remained, taut and sonorous, between the parish and the island. The uncertain wind strayed among them and plucked a defeated music.

The action of one boy was like a very slow dance. He advanced and retreated, leaned sideways to look at his face in a rockpool, pirouetted on a red tassel of seaweed, left deliberately patterned footprints on a patch of sand. He behaved quite unselfconsciously, as though nobody existed on the shore of Birsay but himself that morning. Where the sea had been minutes before he took his slow grave dance. He turned sideways and bent down. His face glittered in the light of a pool.

The old monk who waited for them had never moved in the last hour. He stood above the high-water mark, watching the boys crossing over. He still held his parchment in his hand.

The tall handsome red-headed boy chafed at the slowness of the waters. Several times he clicked his tongue impatiently. He looked towards the island more often than the others. A man with a hawk on his fist came from the courtyard to the edge of the low cliff. The boy's eyes burned. He stood up to his knees in the sea. 'Valt,' he cried, 'Valt.' The falconer let on not to hear but he took the hood from the hawk's head. 'Why didn't you send the boat across for us?' shouted the boy. The hawk heard. It swung its fierce eye round. It fluttered on the tight fist, then shook upwards and free. It was a part of the air, an intense gray upborne concentration. It hung on the wind. It swung between cliff and sea. It eased itself down, and down. It fluttered on to the bare clenched fist of the boy, and rooted itself there. 'Warlock, sweet Warlock,' whispered the boy to the fierce head. Up to his thighs in the sea, he looked round at the others. Only the small dark boy who had a while back been concerned about the seal met his eye. Their mouths relaxed. The teeth of the red-headed boy shone. He held his hawk up high, a proud offering, into the sun.

'You may all cross over now,' said a pedantic voice. They looked across. The old monk had come down to meet them. He stood in the seaweed no more than ten yards from them. 'Come along, please,' he said. 'Enough of the morning has been wasted.'

The boys converged on the old man, swaying in the seaweed, splashing through the last rockpools, scrambling over wet stones. They stood before him at last, shy and smiling, except for the boy with the dark stains on his face and feet.

'A harp,' said the monk. 'A hawk. I think no provision is made for hawks and harps in this school. At least not to begin with. I will consult his grace. Follow me, please.'

The boys followed him up the warm sand. Under the cliff he turned and faced them again. 'Now first,' he said, 'I will show you your dormitory. I will explain the rules and regulations. Stop snivelling, boy. You had to leave your mother sometime. Now follow me up.'

The seal cry came from a cave mouth in the north of the island.

At the cliff-top the instructor gathered the boys round him once more. 'My name is Brother Colomb,' he said. 'Colomb, that means dove. If you don't attend to your lessons however you'll find that I'm anything but a dove. I have a leather tawse that has been hardened in the fire. It has tamed three genera-tions of boys. It has warmed a thousand backsides . . . That is the chapel over there. We'll visit it first of all. You'll be none the worse of a prayer or two.'

Six boys followed Brother Colomb into the porch of the chapel.

'The bishop is wanting to see you all,' Brother Colomb said. 'But later. Just now he is writing in his study. You, boy, take off your cap. Remember where you are. What's your name?'

The Bishop of Orkney, William – Gulielmus Senex he was to be called much later when he sailed on the Jerusalem voyage, but at this time he was still a young man – sat at his desk writing a letter to the Bishop of Nidaros in Norway. He wrote concerning the state of things, spiritual and temporal, in the islands of the west. He formed the letters with great care and seriousness, but whenever a felicitous Latin phrase occurred to him his mouth relaxed and he sent the quill scurrying over the parchment. Sometimes he stopped to sharpen the point. Sometimes the pen ran dry in the middle of a long balanced period, and then he clicked his tongue with annoyance and dipped the point once more into the stone bowl of ink. He paused after a time to read what he had written:

'The merchant ship *Valiant* of Grimsby is watering and provisioning in Hamnavoe and is due to leave on Thursday for Bergen (God willing) with a cargo of English wool and tin. I had a visit here in Birsay from the skipper Ragnar Matthieson, a civil and upright man as far as I can judge. He gave me much news of Norway and also of England. He has promised to carry this letter eastwards to your grace in Trondheim. One of my tenants, Mans, will deliver it to the ship before she sails – that is, if I speak sweetly to him and put a silver coin into his hand, for he is a complex creature, churlish and dependable.

'I thank God for it, at present this earldom in the west is tranquil. The power and authority of our earl, Thorfinn Sigurdson, is such that for thirty years and more from Shetland to Barra a man may break his bread in peace in the midst of his family and in peace lay him down beside his wife when his labours of the day are over. The people of Orkney know a security and a prosperity that have never been since first the islands were settled by our kinsmen, three hundred years ago.

'Yet my hand shakes with foreboding as I write. I think of what has been, and what may be again.

'The truth is, Earl Thorfinn Sigurdson is old. His black beard is now silver and white and gray. He kept much to his bed last winter, with pains in his joints and difficult breathing. He turns increasingly from listening to sagas and heroic lays. The poets in his Hall have a hungry time. Instead he desires scripture to be read to him. Brother Fergus does this, translating from Latin into the vulgar tongue as best he can. But, happily though this augurs for the soul of the old man, it means ill, in my opinion, for the weal of the earldom.

'Earl Thorfinn Sigurdson, in short, will soon be stretched on his death-bed.

'Do I hear you say, reading this in your palace in Trondheim, "True, but God has blessed his loins with sons"? My lord – let you not think it blasphemy – God has overblessed his loins and the womb of beautiful Ingibiorg his wife, for he has two sons. No doubt but you have seen and spoken with Paul and Erlend in the courts of Norway the time they made their allegiance there eight years ago. They are – both of them, I assure you – good and open-hearted men.

'They are, nevertheless, being two, a threat to the earldom and people. They form as it were the lips of an open wound.

'Our northern tribes, from Finland to Greenland, have distinguished themselves in the eyes of all Christendom (and in pagan times also, before that) with many skills: as sailors, merchants, farmers, skalds, warriors, and perhaps above all as lawmen. The little parliaments and the great sit in Iceland and in Orkney and in Caithness. Hardly a knoll in any parish but has, two or three times in the year, its little knot of passionate and persuasive debaters.

'Yet such is the flaw at the heart of all human skill and endeavour – ever since our first father sank his teeth into the apple – that the most important law of all, that concerning inheritance, makes every death-bed in our part of the world a place of wrangling and dread. The flaw goes right through society, from the highest to the lowest, like a twisted thread in a tapestry.

'For, a king of Norway dies. He has, let us say, three sons. The kingdom, which should (like the Church, though not of the same eternal seamless incorrupt weave) be a heraldic garment, whereunder all the folk find shelter and comfort, is straightway riven in three. A farmer in Shetland has, let us say, seven sons. He dies, that good old tiller of the earth, in the course of nature. His barn goes to this one, his byre to this other, this field to the third, that pasture to the fourth, the house to the fifth, the mill to the sixth, ox and dunghill to the simple-minded seventh.

What was once a good farm, bound together in plenteousness and peace, becomes a nest of envy, greed, recrimination. (They would smash the old one's chamber pot into seven pieces, if they could.) Everywhere the past bequeaths to the present a mutilated inheritance.

'You will therefore appreciate what I mean when I whisper to you, as now, that Thorfinn Earl of Orkney waxes old, and two sons look at each other across his prayer-fast whitening drooping head.

'Thorfinn himself had three brothers to contend with, through many a bloody winter, before (the three eldest being dead) he was able to put salves on the wounds of his earldom. And no sooner had these pustules and scabs begun to heal, than a subtle generous handsome nephew came out of the east to claim his father's share. There were more terrible burnings and blood-lettings before that young upstart lay cold among the seaweed of Papa Stronsay.

'The King of Norway grieves, and also smiles, whenever a powerful earl dies out west in the Orkneys. He enters the throne-room with a stricken tear-bright face. The courtiers murmur elegiacally. He rewards the skipper who has brought the news generously – a ring and a gold coin. The court retires to clothe itself in black. The king is alone. He smiles.

'Next morning he orders a room to be prepared. An important guest will no doubt arrive from Orkney in the autumn.

'Now there are two earls over those dangerous islands in the west. It is a recurrent pattern within the history of the north. The king knows that the pattern will work itself out with the inevitability of a saga: confrontation, sword-clash, exile. The defeated earl takes his complaints east across the sea. The king goes down to meet him; kisses him on the shore; draws him among his horses, hawks, tapestries. He sits at the king's fire that winter. The king has many a long earnest secret talk with him. The king offers him money, ships, men. The king says to

him, *You are my man*. He breaks the king's bread. The snow
melts. The birds fly north. The king kisses him farewell at the
shore. The king's ships are suddenly among the islands. Orkney
shrieks again from end to end that summer, a riven harp.

'At the end of another winter of fighting, the king's man sits
weak and alone in the great Hall of Birsay. That Orkney blood-
letting – inflicted once each generation – is necessary for the
health of Norway.

'When I say that Olaf both smiles and grieves at the mis-
fortunes of Orkney, I impute no hypocrisy to him; nor when he
behaves in such a way to the half-earl who seeks a favourable
arbitration (it makes no difference whether the king likes the
suppliant or not). It is simply that, being what he is, the king
cannot act in any other way. He is the hereditary keeper of the
"*pax borealis*". Fate has placed the circle of kingship on his head.
His human face withers between the silver and the bone. From
the moment he sits on the throne his tongue is never again used
for tender, grieving, happy, human words – it is an oracular
organ, making utterance only through rigid precious lips.

'But in the end nothing matters. The chronicler writes his
history in the royal palace, but the saga was conceived and
"finis" put to it before the beginning of time; and soon enough
there will be no one to relish the dark struttings and puppetry of
men, for even the gods, the only creators and begetters, are
doomed to perish.

'Nothing endures. All is consumed in the slow fires of time.
There comes an end to splendour. Kings fare to the ghostly
feast-halls. There is the ancient whisper in the ice: "all noble
lovely things – towers, ships, harps, swords – will fail at last" . . .
This must come. Fate has decreed it. The glories of the earth will
return to ashes and silence.

'Fabric and folding are dust almost at once. Silver flares up, a
brief white flame. Jewels burn aeons-long, slow cold fires; and
then burn out.

'Our history and our thought and art are steeped in this manic melancholy, out of which only one virtue comes – a kind of stoical courage.

'Now, and for a short while only, the sun is above and the sword-arm of the king has strength in it. He can turn his flesh and blood into a few heroic words in a saga (though the words were written down by Fate before the beginning of things). Once each generation the keeper of "*pax borealis*" gathers his royal coat-of-empire about him – it is his war-cloak now – and leads men from Iceland, Faroe, Shetland, Orkney, Caithness, Strathnaver, the Hebrides, Man, into the south. Then for a terrible summer all of western Europe is guled and branded.

'The malcontents and adventurers of Scandinavia are thereby given an overplus of what they most desire, blood and gold . . . Much more important, those half-mutinous princelings in the west learn two important lessons at the same time: glory and obedience.

'The king is the generous giver of rings then. The silver cup goes from mouth to mouth among the warriors. The lips of the skalds are unlocked – they put upon these corrupt fragments of time, battles and sieges, the hardness and polish of jewels.

'The king can forget for a while, in the sun of France, the ancient evil whisper of the ice.

'This is the heroic way for the king to keep his empire together. But war is expensive of men and gold. A war-cruise like that is possible only once in a generation. At other times the earldom of Orkney must be handled with subtlety and cunning: with promises, suggestions, favours, bribes: with the secret passage of spies across the sea: with the skilful deploying (as the earl grows old) of ambition against assurance, of upstart against heir; so that the salutary wound is never allowed to close.

'The question of Orkney causes much anxiety always to the man who wears the very ancient rune-scrawled heraldry of

Scandinavia (and yet it need not, for that problem was resolved before it was stated).

'Outside my window I can see a poor woman. She stoops at a rockpool now. Her fingers go like roots among whelks and pebbles. She is hungry. Her sight is beginning to fail (she has webs at her eyes, she comes occasionally to our little infirmary here to have them washed and bandaged). She sleeps in any old ditch. Yet Mary and her man who wander between flood and ebb have more freedom than the King of Norway.

'The principal task of the Church in these parts, as I see it, is to reinterpret Fate to those fate-ridden tribes of the north. It is true: the actions of men and nations seem to be prompted, rounded, sealed by a sombre inscrutable world-will. Our sagas are obsessed with it. Love and heroism and feasting are enacted in a wintry light: all enter at last the solstice, the heart of darkness . . . But we who stand at the altars of Christ see history across a broken tomb. Time for us is refreshed with perpetual dewfall and bird-song. April is the beginning and end of the circle, and the point of renewal.

'The Earl Thorfinn was not well this morning when I went into his chamber with a psalter to read to him. No food would remain in his stomach. The physician recommended wine. The earl sent the flagon away. He seemed like any old man who is sick, that is to say, he is like a spoiled, petulant, frightened boy. I think he did not know who I was. He asked for Brother Fergus. But even the holy words are a burden to him now. He kissed Brother Fergus' hands. Brother Fergus sat in silence with him for an hour.

'Soon we are to have, once more, what we most dread – a divided earldom here in Orkney.

'Brother Colomb, that good old pedant, came to me this morning waving a scrap of parchment. He seemed to be quite excited. It proved to be a list of the names of the boys who are coming here to be educated by the monks. Brother Colomb pointed to two names with a forefinger that shook perceptibly: Hakon Paulson and Magnus Erlendson: the two future earls of Orkney. All the seven new boys are due to enrol this morning, as soon as the waters part for them. Perhaps they are here already. They will reside in the monastery for two years at least.

'They have come to us, Brother Colomb truly remarked, in the time of their innocency, when the soul is most open to divine instruction. The brothers will do their best, of course, to teach them Latin, mathematics, etc.; but we in Birsay will have a very grievous thing to answer for if we cannot demonstrate to those innocents that at last, even under our cold northern sun, Fate has lately woven for itself a garment of immortal beauty.

'Your grace must forgive me – my letters become at last a graveyard of images: harps, coats, jewels. I will resurrect one more image, then I will be silent (except to ask for your continual blessing upon the people of Orkney).

'Hakon Paulson and Magnus Erlendson, then, are coming here like the two lips of a dynastic wound. We will see what a little ghostly surgery can do.'

After they had left their baggage in the dormitory, each beside his own bed, and knelt together in the chapel for a while, the boys were herded into the large classroom beside the sea. There they gave particulars about themselves to Brother Colomb; who wrote their names and their fathers' names and the names of their fathers' estates in the book, piecing the fragments and incoherencies together as best he could.

Three monks walked past the arched window, carrying over their heads, upturned, a skin boat from the haddock fishing; from the fist of one monk hung a bright bunch of fish.

The boy who had carried his harp across the ebb said that his name was Sigurd. His father was called Kali. Kali had the farm of The Bu in the island of Hoy. His mother and three sisters also lived there. Also there were fifteen servants, all women. He had left The Bu that morning. All the women had come down to the beach to wave farewell to him. His three sisters stood there dabbing their eyes in their aprons.

'Sigurd Kalison,' said Brother Colomb gravely, 'this is a place of men entirely. You'll miss the little sisters and the women. There's not much chatter on this island.'

'It will make a good change, Brother,' said Sigurd Kalison.

The tall red-headed boy on whose fist the hawk had flown said there was surely no need on his part to say much. Everybody knew him. He had often visited the island and whenever he did he stayed at the Hall. Did Brother Colomb really want him to say more? The monastery had known him since the day he had been held up at the font. Very well, since it was necessary. His name was Hakon Paulson. His father's name was Paul Thorfinnson. The father of Paul was Thorfinn Sigurdson. Thorfinn Sigurdson was Earl of Orkney. Thorfinn's father had been Sigurd Hlodverson, Earl of Orkney. The father of Sigurd the earl—

'That's enough,' said Brother Colomb. 'All the boys are equal in this island. You will not be allowed to keep a hawk.'

The cry of the stricken seal mingled with the noises of wind and sea.

The boy with freckles and hair the colour of pale honey, he who had tested the cold of the rockpool, said that his name was Hold. His lips trembled on the utterance of his father's name. Brother Colomb said gently that Hold would have to say who his father was; it was necessary for the enrolment. Hold said that his father had been called Ragnar. Colomb asked if Ragnar was dead. Hold said that Ragnar his father had died in the winter. He had had the estate of Ness in the Hebrides. He was buried in a small island there. Colomb asked Hold if he thought he would be happy in the Orkneys. Hold shook his head. He said that he did not think he would like it.

The fishermen-monks began in the chapel, a low murmur, to thank God for His gift of fish.

The boy with the mass of black curls said that his name was Havard Gunison. He was called by his mother's name, Guni. Everybody, he said, was of the opinion that his father was a useless kind of a man. It was thought to be unlucky to inherit the name of a man like that. At all events, his father's name was no part of his name. His father had a farm near Hamnavoe. It had never been good farmland in the first place, all bog and granite. The estate had not got any better under his father. His father's name was Arni. Arni sat at the fire all winter playing chess with cattlemen and sailors, whoever would sit down with him. It was said that his father had not had a weapon in his hand for twenty years. His mother Guni was on the other hand a purposeful woman. She had managed so far to keep the farm together, and wring a crop out of the fields at the end of every summer, and enough cheese and milk and ale to keep them going. Everybody in the neighbourhood admired Guni very much. They thought it right that he should be called by his mother's name: Havard Gunison.

'He seems to be a philosopher, your father,' said Brother Colomb. 'Think well of him sometimes. We could do with a few more of his kind in the north.'

Down at the shore a young voice began to call and cajole.

The boy with the wet shoes and feet said (between sneezes) that his name was Sighvat. His father was called Sokk. His father had a small farm in Westray, and three ships. He was a merchant. Some people said that his father was a Viking, but that was not true, he was a merchant. A grieve looked after the farm. His father was at home all winter. Then he and his men drank a good deal. In spring, after the sowing, he sailed south again in his three ships. Sokk had a licence from the earl to trade as far as Ireland and Cornwall. Sokk would be setting forth again in about ten days' time. The shepherds and ploughmen had been caulking the ships for a week past on the foreshore. His mother, Sokk's wife, was rather sad all summer. But then when Sokk came home again before harvest he generally brought with him fine linen in the holds, and silver arm-bands. He brought combs. Then the women of Westray admired themselves for days in the pools.

The boy wheezed and coughed and dabbed his eyes. 'Salt water is wholesome water. You can dry your feet later at the refectory fire,' said Brother Colomb.

The stonework shook. The sky outside was a surge of blue and white. The wind was rising.

The boy whose progress across the ebb had been a slow lingering dance spoke so softly that Brother Colomb could not hear what he said, though he bent forward and enlarged his ear with his hand. The boy's lips fluttered, a few soft syllables issued, silk clippings. Brother Colomb said that either the bees had made wax in his old ears or the boy was trying to out-dove him. 'Think of a trumpet, and then speak,' said Brother Colomb. 'Imagine you are shouting into that gale outside.' The boy breathed deeply and opened his mouth a little wider. Then the listeners could distinguish a spirant at least – the name of the boy was either 'Flan' or 'Finn' or 'Flos'. At last Brother Colomb established definitely that it was Finn. And that his father's name was Thorkel. And that his father had a farm at Kirbister in Orphir. The boy's lips fluttered and were still. 'Ah well,' said Brother Colomb, 'I suppose, Finn Thorkelson, there is too much loudness in this world.'

Brother Colomb put old faint breath across the enrolment parchment. The ink dulled.

'You will be pleased to hear,' he said, 'that now you are going to have something to eat. That's all boys think about anyway, their bellies. There's grilled trout and ale – so Brother Paul says, he's the cook this week. After that the serious business of this school begins. In the evening you are to have your first lesson. Before you leave the monastery in two years' time I hope that you'll be adequate in most subjects – reading, writing, music,

Latin, mathematics. You'll have all the time in the world for fishing, chess, verse-making, sailing, swimming, cliff climbing. The most important thing of all for you to learn is this – how to bear yourselves courteously among all men everywhere, in a manner pleasing to God.'

The wind carried a boy's voice from the edge of the sea. Brother Colomb flashed a look at his pupils, then at the drying parchment on his desk. 'There should be another boy,' he said. 'There are seven names down for enrolment. How is it that there are only six of you in this classroom?'

'There was a boy who wouldn't come in,' said Hold Ragnarson. 'He left us among the rocks. He walked across to a cave.'

Brother Colomb went to the tall arched window. He leaned out. He shouted, 'Boy . . . You out there . . . What are you doing? . . . You are to come in at once to be enrolled.'

They heard whistles and snatches of song from the rocks.

'He's whistling to the seals,' said Brother Colomb. 'Do any of you know who that boy is?'

Four of the boys shook their heads. 'I know him,' said Hakon Paulson. 'I know him very well, of course. He's my cousin Magnus Erlendson from Paplay.' The boy smiled: he remembered rockpools in the sun, a cage of doves, small flung fists and tears and reconciliation.

Brother Colomb turned again to the window. 'Boy,' he called, 'come here. I need to speak to you. I know who you are. You are wasting my time and the time of the school.'

There was silence outside. They heard the rattle of feet on pebbles. The wind surged and fell away. They heard a whisper of feet across the salty grass. 'It's too dark in there,' said the voice. 'I won't come inside today. There's a seal hurt, down at the rock. Didn't you hear him crying out? I'm trying to reach him, but I can't till it ebbs a bit more.'

'Tell me your name,' said Brother Colomb quietly, leaning out.

There was a silence. Then the hidden mouth said, 'Names are wrong. Men are imprisoned in their names. Angels and animals don't need names. I do not like my name. It means "great, powerful". I don't want to be great and powerful. The world is sick because of people wanting to be great and powerful.'

'That's true,' said the old monk, leaning so far out that the wind lifted and sifted his few silver hairs. 'But the name was given to you in holy baptism, and so it is a seal put by God upon your life.'

'I do not like it,' said the boy.

'There is another kind of greatness and power,' said Brother Colomb seriously. 'There are the heroes of the spirit . . . At least tell me the names of your parents.'

'My mother Thora lives in Paplay in Holm,' said the boy. 'My father is called Erlend. I suppose some day he'll be the Earl of Orkney.'

The tall red-headed boy, the falconer, Hakon Paulson, shouted suddenly, 'That's a lie! It's my father Paul – he's to be Earl of Orkney. Paul is the elder son of Earl Thorfinn. Magnus's father is simply my father's brother. That counts for nothing.' . . . His young face was white and tense and quivering among the candles.

'Be quiet!' said Brother Colomb sharply. 'This is a place of silence. Here nobody shouts like that.'

Hakon Paulson gnawed his lip. The wondering faces of the boys turned from his guttering rage towards the window that was all a silent driven tumult of blue and white. They stood on tiptoe but the ledge was too high for them; they could not see the blithe disobedient face on the other side. The window blazed with a single white cloud.

Brother Colomb sent another appeal into the wind and sun. 'Won't you come in, great and powerful one, and meet your fellow-pupils?'

'Not till the seal is well,' said the boy. 'Somebody has hit him with an axe. No hunting should be allowed on this island at all.'

The wind hurled gulls about the sky.

Hakon Paulson approached the window again. 'Brother Colomb,' he said, 'I have a certain influence with Erlendson. I'm his cousin. I'm sure I can persuade him to come in. We understand one another. But if he refuses I could easily put my hands on him and drag him into the school. With your permission. I'm very strong.'

'You will stay where you are,' said Brother Colomb.

A bell beat softly once, and sent bronze tremblings down the corridor. Brother Colomb turned away from the window. 'You will go in to dinner now,' he said. 'It seems this truant will only come in when he is ready.'

Brother Colomb was left alone in the classroom. Sealight glittered high on one wall. The monk heard distant commiseration under the crags, then laughter, then singing. The sea had ebbed now very far out and a waste of tangles and rocks and pools lay under the evening light. The lips of the old man moved. He crossed himself. The boy and the seal had met at last. A surge of wind brought every syllable of the greeting into the classroom.

> Come from the rock now, cold one.
> See, I have a fish for you in my hand.
> My name is Magnus.
> I have told the hunters to leave this shore.
> There's a wound in your head.
> If you do not come to me soon you will die.
> You'll be colder than shells.
> Rats and crabs will cover your beautiful coat.

When Bishop William came to welcome the new class to Birsay before the Latin lesson began that evening, Magnus Erlendson was sitting with red hands among the other boys.

Song of Battle

In the Menai Strait, between Wales and the island of Anglesey, two ships manoeuvred slowly against one another. They were plated with shields, they bristled with arrows and axes and swords.

The ship tacking south was crammed with a host of northerners: Norwegians, Danes, Hebrideans, Icelanders, Orkneymen. A man sat in the stern with an ice-coloured mask over his brow and cheekbones. The King of Norway's bodyguard stood about him.

Mans the peasant from Revay Hill in Birsay laboured at the rowing bench. His clenched fists made circles. His oar rose and fell. He sweated. His face went from bilgewater to the gulls above the mast, then back again to the swilter and glug of foul water among the bottomboards. 'Faster,' shouted the master oarsman. Mans thought of Hild, and his few acres, and Prem's loom and ale-kirn, and the heart fluttered in him like a caught bird. He was very frightened indeed. His blade sank deeper into the water. He could hear shouts in a strange language. The archers began to gather in the well of the *Sea Eagle*. Mans did not know what was happening, but the taste of danger and death was in his mouth.

A horn rasped from the stern. A high chant rose above the sound of gulls and sea-surge: *Men in the Welsh ship*! The oars beat on. A response came back, tremulous, thin, purified by the waters, *We are listening, strangers.* It was a ritualistic dialogue, a prelude to battle. Mans' shoulders creaked. The Norse herald

pitched his voice higher: *The channel is narrow, Welshman.
There's not room for two ships to pass.* The answer came at once,
Turn round then. Back with you to the whales and mermaids. This
was mockery and poetry too. Laughter passed from the Welsh
ship to the Norse ship. Mans heard one or two random shouts,
'The channel belongs to us!' . . . 'This is Menai, yes indeed, and
we are Welshmen!' . . . 'Get home with you, sea wolves.'

Archers fitted arrows into bows.

The ritual contest of voices went on. *What men have come
down from the north today? We have a chronicler on the ship and
he wants to know. So that the names may be carved on a
gravestone at the shore . . . Great heroes: Vidkunn, Sigurd, Serk,
Dag, Skop, Ogmund. Finn. Thord. Eyvind. Kali. Hakon. Magnus.
Hold. Sigurd. They feed the ravens. They shake the sun from their
shields. What is the name of the land behind you? . . . Anglesey, a
fair and a holy island . . .*

Mans looked beyond his raised dripping oar. There was a
beach over there indeed, and women standing here and there
among the rocks. The Norse voice intoned, *We will land there,
for corn and women . . .* The response then, *We welcome you to
Anglesey in the Welsh fashion . . .* The first arrows fell into the
Sea Eagle then; they hissed down, they struck here and there,
they clung and quivered at thwart and deck. An oarsman two
benches in front of Mans sagged and slumped. Mans saw, with
horror, an arrow sticking out of the man's neck. Then with a
high blithe harp-like sound the rank of archers in the *Sea Eagle*
released a first volley. 'Faster,' shouted the master oarsman.
Mans had never seen such a thing before. His mouth was dry.
He lurched back and fore on the thwart with dead shoulders,
but his oar too sang in the sea. The music of battle was getting
louder.

The dead oarsman was dragged from the thwart.

The heraldic voices crossed once more. *Welshmen, listen. You
have killed Arn the weaver. He lived at Yell in Shetland . . . It will*

be a ragged winter in Shetland then, but not so cold as for Arn . . .
He was a humorous man, this Welsh herald. The young Norse
nobles laughed, standing here and there about the ship, testing
axes on thumbs. The archers stepped forward again, with taut
poised bows. *Archers,* cried the Norse herald, *argue with them,
my tongue is tired.* The arrows left the ship like rapturous birds.
Then, a few seconds later, Mans heard the screaming of Welshmen.

Some of the King's bodyguards were pointing towards the
bow of the *Sea Eagle.* The king stood up. Mans could see how
moved the king was under his silver mask. Mans stole a
moment from swinging the oar to look over his shoulder. A
young man in a white linen wine-stained shirt was sitting in the
bow. He was holding a book, of all things. His lips moved, his
fingers slowly unrolled the writing. *They have eaten sour grapes,*
he read aloud from the psalter, *and now the teeth of the children
are set on edge.* Mans saw that the young man was Magnus
Erlendson, the son of one of the Orkney earls. The King yelled
at Magnus Erlendson from the stern, but his voice was lost in
the rising din of battle.

Meantime the young Norsemen had put aside their bows and
were balancing the long delicate spears shoulder high. They
formed a rank in the well of the ship. One young man bent
down first and tied the thong of his shoe (it does not do to make
slovenly entry at the door of death).

Mans added a brief ragged stroke to the onsurge on the ship.

The master oarsman called for the port oars to be shipped.
Mans dragged his oar in and set it, sklintering with sea, along
the thwart. The helmsman swung the ship round. Mans saw the
Welsh ship, a few yards away, heaving and dipping. She bristled
with spears. Mans saw the rank of Welsh spearsmen with spears
drawn back shoulder high. He had never seen such savagery and
splendour. He put his terrified head on his knees. All about him
then was splintering wood and the shrieks of men.

The *Sea Eagle* staggered in the water.

The herald's voice rose above the bedlam, *You have killed Finn and Thord, farmers in Iceland . . . Finn and Thord* (came the response) *will cultivate seaweed this summer . . .*

Then the ship seemed to rise in the water as the spears left her in a long *swoosh.*

Well hunted, hawks, cried the Welsh herald.

The falconry has only begun, little birds, sang the Norse herald.

The ships circled each other, warily, as though neither of them was over-eager for the feast of blood.

The enemies could see each other's faces now, calm or terrified or twisted with rage. The Earl of Shrewsbury looked across the cold gulf at the King of Norway. The King of Norway looked back at Hugh Earl of Shrewsbury. He asked one of his bodyguard to pass him his bow, the one with the silver-and-ivory studs. Another member of the royal body-guard, Oswald Helgelander, the captain of the archers, was already fitting his arrow. 'I think it would not be difficult,' he said to the King, 'for a passable archer to strike that dom-inating man in the stern of their ship.' 'We will try both together,' said the King, and twanged the string of his bow – 'we will see which of us can kill him.' . . . 'Who is he?' asked Hakon Paulson of Orkney, his voice shaking with joy, looking across at the Welsh earl.

The Norse herald took up Hakon Paulson's question and flung it across to the herald in the Welsh ship. *Who is the dark ugly man sitting on the high thwart? . . . That is Hugh the Proud, Earl of Shrewsbury . . . This is strange. We have come all this way to talk to a man by the name of Hugh . . . No, but tell me this, who is the fat man on board your ship, the man who is hiding there behind a ring of swords, the man playing at bows-and-arrows, the one with the silver mask? . . . The King of Norway is in these parts . . . Some kings are a long time getting home. The queen watches. The sea is empty . . . The Welshman has a bitter tongue. We will*

soon speak face to face . . . Now it is axes, Norseman . . .
Welshman, now it is swords and axes and fire . . .

The hull of the *Sea Eagle* quivered. The ships had kissed and
fallen apart again. Mans thrust his head between his knees.
'God,' he whispered, 'get me safe out of this and I'll never say a
wrong word to Hild again. Blessed Mary, I'll go to Mass every
Sunday. I'll be good to the poor folk who come begging round
the doors. I will. I promise.'

Feet kicked at Mans' shoulders. He thought the hour of his
death had come. The feet passed over him. He opened his eyes
and looked up. A half-naked man stood above him, on the hull,
and held a grappling-iron. All along that side of the ship men
waited with grappling-irons. Between the men with the grappling-irons long spears thrust back the Welsh axe-men. The
battle was now one high wavering scream. Mans saw that his
fellow-oarsmen were gathering in the well and spitting on their
axes. It seemed to be safer there. Hardly any Welsh weapons were
falling into the ship now; only an occasional futile arrow. Mans
got to his feet. He took his axe from his belt. He put a tremulous
kiss on the blade. He moved over among his fellow-oarsmen.

Magnus Erlendson was still unrolling the psalter in the bow
as if it was Evensong in the Birsay church.

The grappling-irons fell on the Welsh ship with a clang. They
fell and clutched like iron claws.

The first Norseman leapt into the Welsh ship and was cut
down at once. The prodding spears from the *Sea Eagle* held the
Welshmen back. Six more Norsemen leapt the gap. The ships
rose and fell and rasped on each other.

The Earl of Shrewsbury was urging his men on. He raged at
them. He offered them showers of gold. He reminded them that
their names would be mentioned in the poem that a mountain
bard would compose about their victory. 'Drive the wolves from
your sacred hearths!' he cried. The Welshmen took heart. They
fell upon the six Norwegians and cut them to pieces.

The King of Norway and Oswald Helgelander looked carefully at Hugh the Proud; they tilted their heads; they narrowed their eyes at him. There was a consultation of guardsmen. Arrows were passed to the King and Oswald. They raised their bows shoulder high. They held their bows like harps. The arrows sang from their shoulders.

Twelve Norsemen dropped into the Welsh ship, and then five more. Their raised axes glinted in the sun. Their axes fell.

The master oarsman said to the oarsmen in the well of the ship. 'Are you all ready? It'll soon be our turn.'

Another qualm went through Mans.

His fellow oarsmen were laughing all about him, their feet were restless, they yelled derision at the enemy. They seemed to be eager for the taste of blood. But more of the whites of their eyes were showing than the blue.

A score of Norsemen surged up and across and staggered to their feet under the sail with the red dragon sewn on it. Celtic cries mingled with Norse cries, one cold tremulous rant. More Norsemen passed over. 'Get ready,' said the master oarsman. Mans added his shout to the jargon.

In the middle of every battle there is a still moment, when it seems that the swords hang suspended in the air and the enemies make stone gestures at one another. That moment – the eye of the battle – occurred now. Through the silence Mans heard a voice: *Who is this that cometh from Edom, with dyed garments from Bosra, this beautiful one in his robe, walking in the greatness of his strength? . . .* He turned. Magnus Erlendson was standing up in the bow, and he was reading words out of his psalter. 'He has been there all the time,' thought Mans. It was a dangerous place to stand. Three Welsh arrows were sticking awry out of the strake where Magnus Erlendson leaned with his scroll. Indeed some weapon must have brushed him; there was a smear of blood on his forehead. He intoned quietly, *Thou preparest a table before me*

in the presence of my enemies. Thou anointest my head with oil.
My cup runneth over . . .

A terrible wail rose up from the Welsh ship and drowned the singing of Magnus Erlendson.

The Earl of Shrewsbury had been wounded, and grievously. An arrow was sticking out of his face: his right eye and his mouth were in ruins. He spat out a few red teeth into his hand. Then slowly he began to sink to his knees. The Welsh guardsmen caught him by the arms and shoulders. They held him up, as if they could keep their leader alive by speaking sweet gentle consoling words to him; as if death could come to no man so long as he stood on his feet and faced across at his enemies. 'Dear one,' the guardsmen murmured, 'dear leader, the victory is ours.' His mouth was one thick gule. Then a second arrow struck the Earl of Shrewsbury on the face: it shattered nose-plate and nose and passed on into his skull. The body was borne backwards by the impact. It passed out of the hands of his guardsmen. It fell among the Welsh oarsmen. They flung the blood and brains and bone splinters from them, and screamed. The Earl clattered on the deck and lay awry there. At once the whole Welsh host understood that their leader was dead. A terrible cry arose.

The King of Norway raised his bow in the air. He laughed. He himself had killed the Welsh leader. He had turned the tide of battle, as a great king should. His guardsmen smiled all round him. Oswald Helgelander bowed to the King, acknowledging that it was the King's arrow and not his that had given the death-wound. (But privately Oswald Helgelander had his doubts about that: it seemed to him that the King's arrow had been badly flighted and had fallen into the sea, whereas his own had hurtled true from face to face.) 'Your arrow was the arrow,' he said. The King clapped his hands. The upper part of his face was fixed and silver like the northern sun; but he laughed out of broken teeth and shaking russet beard.

The Norsemen could pass unhindered now from one ship to the other. They passed across in order. Their axes rose. Their axes glittered for a moment in the sun. Their axes fell. The Welshmen retreated before them. The deck of the Welsh ship was slippery with blood. They formed a ring about the body of Hugh the Proud. They gestured with their swords. The Norse axes rose and glittered and fell. The Welshmen formed a shrinking circle about their dead war-man.

The King called for a cup of wine to be passed round. 'Magnus,' he said, 'pour out some of the red French wine.' (He had appointed Magnus Erlendson to be his cupbearer at the beginning of the voyage.) 'Where is Magnus?' Then he remembered. He looked the length of the empty *Sea Eagle* and saw Magnus leaning against the mast, still slowly unrolling the parchment with the black and scarlet ruck of letters on it. The lips of the young man moved soundlessly.

'Oswald Helgelander,' said the King, 'you see to the wine. I have never known behaviour like that in a battle before.'

The battle was almost over. Less than a dozen Welshmen stood about the faceless Hugh. There were more Norsemen looting the cabins and stripping the dead than there were at the ritual of the axe-fall. Another Welshman went down on his knees.

Mans judged that it would be safe enough now to jump aboard the Welsh ship. At any rate he would have played some part in the battle, not like that Magnus Erlendson who had done nothing all day but sing psalms. He gave a wild yell and leapt into the Welsh ship with his axe raised. He slipped in a pool of blood. He fell on his backside among a strewment of corpses. Swords and axes passed over him. Mans lay there as if he was dead.

The Welsh herald and the Norse herald met under the tattered red sail of the Welsh ship. While the battle lasted they had not been able to make themselves heard. No warrior had made a pass against those sacred inviolate mouths. Their necks crossed. They embraced. They spoke, but their words were not the conversation of ordinary men: they uttered formal well-turned phrases.

I greet thee well, said the Welshman. *Thou hast come down from the ice in a lucky time.*

I greet thee well also, said the Norseman. *We have had a brave reception in Wales.*

It has been a great battle. The poet on the mountain will make a song about this.

It will be spoken of round winter fires in Iceland.

Great and splendid and victorious warriors have come out of the north.

Fate decreed the outcome: otherwise the brave Celts would have won the day.

Who is the young man who has fought this battle for you with a psalter?

He is Magnus, the son of Erlend, the son of Thorfinn, the son of Sigurd, the son of Ragnvald, great and mighty earls. Death is proud to have such heroes in his keeping.

Sigurd Kalison passed the heralds, going up to the king's cabin to drink from the silver cup. It seemed as if his axe was wound in torn filthy red silk. Sigurd had heard the heralds speak of Magnus. He said to them, 'There is a coward in every battle.' Drops of blood fell from his axe. He passed on. He strode from deck to deck. He raised his axe to the silver mask above.

'All the same,' said the Welsh herald in his ordinary voice, 'a coward wouldn't be sitting in the very teeth of the swords.'

The sun sank beyond Ireland.

Hakon Paulson passed the heralds, going up to the king's cabin to drink from the engraved cup. He turned and saw Magnus Erlendson brooding over his book. He smiled and said, 'Magnus' and raised his hand. Magnus looked at him gravely.

Hakon Paulson, still smiling, leapt up the three steps to the royal cabin in one bound.

The Welsh herald said, *I think we have spoken overmuch today. My tongue is heavy.*

The Norse herald answered, *It will come to silence soon enough.*

The Welsh herald said, *Now I must do a bitter thing. I must make acknowledgement of our defeat to your King.*

The last living Welshman except himself, who was sacrosanct, had leapt overboard and was swimming towards the Anglesey shore. He swam through corpses and broken spears and a thin scum of red. He made for a wailing beach. Among the rocks of the island the women were setting up a long savage keen.

> Our curse upon the bright haired strangers.
> May the agony they have brought to
> > Wales return upon their heads.
> A torrent of blood to turn their millstones.
> Wives, mothers, sweethearts of
> > Orkney
> Remember this day
> When you go among wounds and ghosts,
> When foreign horsemen sleep in your barns.

It grew darker. Magnus Erlendson rolled up his psalter. He tied it with a linen thread.

The master oarsman ordered his men to set the Welsh ship on fire. The twilight was dappled then with torches going in procession from ship to ship. Flaring tongues were thrust at the sail and under thwarts and among the cook's butter and oil. Mans went with his torch here and there about the deck. He had never seen such a feast of death. The flames made everything look like a carnival; the dead warriors lay here and there like men glutted with revelry. He unpinned an opal-and-silver brooch from the coat of one of the Welsh captains. 'You won't be needing this in the morning,' said Mans. He heard the clang of retracted grappling-irons. 'Back aboard,' yelled the master oarsman. Mans put the brooch in his breeches pocket and leapt between the two decks. He would give this piece of loot to Hild. It would prove that he was as much a hero as the best of them.

A lonely figure stood in the bow of the *Sea Eagle* in the darkness.

The young Orkney warriors stood about the King and drank one after another from the silver cup. It was their turn, after the Hebrideans. The throat of Hakon Paulson convulsed. Sigurd Kalison touched the white rim thrice with his mouth. Havard Gunison folded and refolded his tongue in the red delicious silk. A few drops fell from the replete mouth of Hold Ragnarson on to his wounded hand; he cried out with the pain. Sighvat Sokk merely lipped the silver; he shuddered; wine did not agree with him. Finn Thorkelson's face was eclipsed for a moment with the precious chalice of victory.

An Icelander took the cup from him. The Orkneymen moved back. Other Icelanders crowded about the King. Oswald Helge-lander emptied a new flagon into the cup. Now it was the turn of the Icelanders.

Mans snored under his rowing bench. The other oarsmen slept all about him, except one who had been wounded in the chest. Mans dreamed that he was home in Orkney, and he was pouring out on the table from a casket a shower of pearls and coins. But Hild instead of being pleased stood weeping in the open door.

The king of Norway stood among his heroes. He held the cup. 'It seems to me,' he said, 'that there was a battle fought here-abouts today.' He had taken off his mask. The silver and crimson reflections of the wine cup undulated across his broad pockmarked face.

They laughed all about him.

'It seems to me,' said the King, 'that we have won a great victory.'

The warriors roared and clapped their hands and stamped their feet.

'But there is no victory,' said the King, 'where no defeat has been acknowledged.'

There was a sudden silence.

The curtain at the cabin door was drawn aside. The black-cloaked Welsh herald stood there. He approached the King. He knelt and kissed the King's hand. *The Menai Strait is yours, King. A golden thunderbolt has fallen on Wales. Thy queen will see thee, Norway. Thou wilt show her thy crown with a new precious jewel in it.*

The King smiled. He nodded to Paul Breck. Paul his chancellor took a leather purse from his belt and opened it and shook out three silver pieces into the palm of the Welsh herald.

The King said, 'I drink to the valour of Wales.' He raised the cup.

The Welsh herald rose and bowed to the King. He turned. The Norsemen saw his tears then and his face moving with grief. The curtain was drawn back. The Welshman passed out into the darkness.

'The victory!' shouted the Icelanders and the Orkneymen and the Hebrideans and the Danes and the Faroese and the Norwegians. 'The victory!'

The King drank deeply. He set the cup down on the table. The warriors left off cheering when they saw the downcurve of his mouth and the double vertical furrow in his brow.

He pointed to the cabin door: beyond which was silence.

'Fetch Magnus Erlendson,' he said. 'Before any more is done we have things to say to that young man.'

Sigurd Kalison and Hold Ragnarson found Magnus with the sleeve torn from his shirt. He was kneeling beside the white and red torso of the wounded oarsman. The man groaned and whispered. The fingers of Magnus Erlendson went skilfully between the broken flesh and the unfolding linen.

In the morning the *Sea Eagle* was in the Irish Sea, sailing south towards Scilly and the coasts of France. The oars rose and fell.

The herald stood on the deck.

Three horns blorted.

A proclamation from the hand of the King of Norway to the princes and chiefs of the west.

Now all the islands to the north and west of Britain are under the hand of Norway, from Faroe to Scilly; and Orkney is the chiefest earldom among these. We confirm that our servant Paul Thorfinnson is Earl of Orkney and that his brother Erlend Thorfinnson is Earl of Orkney also. May they govern long in our peace and favour. And we declare further that after Paul and Erlend there shall govern in Orkney Hakon son of Paul and Magnus son of Erlend, those two, right leal and sweet and trusty servants, who fought for us in the sea battle at Menai; and are well worthy therefore to be gathered into the one great music of the North.

Mans paused on his stroke, wondering what the high-flown jargon could mean.

'Faster,' shouted the master oarsman.

The Temptations

It was said, concerning the holy martyr Magnus, that to gain his soul's kingdom he had to suffer five grievous temptations, and but that he was upheld then and ever and near the hour of his blessed martyrdom by a certain comforter that was sent to him, his soul might have been overborne by the evil one and brought down into the fires of hell.

This stranger appeared unto Magnus first at the time that the king of Norway was in the Orcades, busking him for a war-cruise as far as Wales and Ireland (but none knew then what the king intended.) Magnus Erlendson was then a young man, and stood betwixt the arch and the king's ship, with the other young men, his companions, waiting on the king's word and command. While the other young men were disputing and laughing at the shore, with their hawks and harps and swords, Magnus stood apart and alone. The stranger came down it seemed to Magnus from the cloister and called him by his name, and said, 'The loom is set for thee now.' Magnus did not by any means understand the man's speech. The man put upon Magnus a look of much sweetness and gravity and said, 'Now that thou art a man, Magnus, thou must weave well upon the loom of the spirit. Thou canst weave whatsoever thou desirest, the white fold of blessedness, or darkness, or Joseph's coat of many colours.' Then Magnus said, 'Tell me thy name.' But the man would only say that he was the keeper of the loom, and that he was sent to guard the soul of Magnus from hurt. 'For,' saith he, 'there is another stranger that will presently appear unto thee, my dark opposite, the tempter. He will come to thee in many subtle disguises. The tempter and I are never far from one another. Nay, we are as close as twins. We wrestle forever upon the mountain of eternity, above the dark vale where dwell the tribes of men. This tempter will contrive if so he can to ruin thy loom, he will seek with many cunning devices to bring thy soul into hell. Look where he cometh now.' Magnus looked and saw approaching him from the door of the great Hall Egil the chamberlain: who saith to Magnus that he brought great tidings. The king (said Egil) had decided on war. He would sail the *Sea Eagle* as far south as Ireland and Wales and Cornwall. Then Magnus asked what innocent throats were like to be cut that summer? And he asked what churches would have stone removed from stone, and what mills were like to be burnt? But Egil said, 'You must sail on the king's ship, Magnus. You are destined to be a hero and a great warrior. The king has done you a particular honour. He has made you his cupbearer, you are to stand at the king's shoulder when he dines on shipboard.' Then Egil gave Magnus an axe for the war-cruise. 'This weapon,' he said, 'will bring you much fame and glory.' Magnus said that Egil should rather bring him a psalter down to the ship. He said that he would follow the king to the wars, for that the king was the anointed servant of God and so it behoved all subjects to obey him. Then, after Egil had departed in much wonderment, the stranger returned and said to the young man, 'The first white threads are in the loom now, Magnus. Your prayers, prayers uttered on your behalf, right actions, blessings put upon you, holy observances, penances, pilgrimages, all will be woven into the immaculate garment.'

Then the stranger bade Magnus go in peace to the war.

March fell, a cold wave of light, over the islands.

It laved the world.

It passed through the bodies of the young men and girls. It left them clean and trembling for love.

The wave surged on. The sun climbed. In April the body of Magnus took a first kindling, blurrings of warmth and light. A slow flush went over his body.

The beasts in the field quenched their black flames, one on another.

The hill was opened by the plough. Fire and earth had their way one with another. Was everywhere the loveliest spurting of seed and egg and spawn.

Girls felt into the rockpool, flowed, climbed out into the sun with sweet silver streaming bodies. They shrieked.

Magnus burned.

Hold Ragnarson's voice in the garden, 'What's wrong, Magnus? I can get you a girl. I know them all.'

Mans left the ox in the furrow. His fist trembled on the latch. Hild inside was baking bread. It was noon. Earth hands mingled with fire hands.

The cold voices in the stone web, *Simile factum est regnus caelorum homini regi qui fecit nuptias filio suo.* A certain king made a great wedding.

Magnus carried his tormented body into the church. Holy water glittered at fingers and forehead. He knelt. He prayed.

The tinkers left the cliff hollows brimming with the crushed smells of seapink, trefoil, daisy.

Hold Ragnarson again. 'What's wrong, Magnus? A young man in your position could have as many girls as he wanted.'

A wedding, then. Some of his friends – Hakon, Sigurd, Finn – were already married. The lusts of men are sanctified with ceremony.

'Magnus, there is a certain girl in Shetland called Ingerth Olafsdotter. Olaf has a large farm there. Ingerth is beautiful, chaste, modest. Think of it, Magnus. You are to be earl here in Orkney one day – there must be children to follow you . . .' The mother's voice – Thora. She had seen the stirrings and burnings in him.

The sun went down. The lovers came out like moths. They tormented one another in the two-tongued invisible flame that burned between them in the first darkness. The mouth of Hold Ragnarson touched a white shoulder. The girl moaned between shame and desire.

At midnight a young man entered the rockpool, a dark solitary flame.

'My lord, the ship left Shetland on Friday, with Ingerth.' . . . Hold Ragnarson's voice in the garden, envious and glad.

The fires of creation. Out of the mingled fires of men and women come new creatures to people the earth. This is a good ordinance of God. A certain king made a marriage feast. 'Magnus, thou art bidden now to the marriage.' . . . 'No, but I cannot come, for that I am myself to be a bridegroom soon.' . . . 'Magnus, thou art bidden to the marriage feast of Christ with his church.' . . . 'No, but I cannot come, for that I have to study statecraft and the duties of a ruler; but I wish well to the ceremony and the guests.' . . . 'Magnus, thou art summoned.' . . . 'No, but I have no suitable clothes to put on. See what I wear on my body – a garment scorched and stained with the burnings of desire.' . . . 'Magnus, there is a coat being woven for thee for the wedding. I have told thee.'

Magnus awoke from the dream. The friend stood no longer in the room. The taste of ashes was in his mouth.

'My lord, Ingerth will leave the ship at noon.'

Contrariwise, the hideous fires of hell, even here on earth: these flame through the bodies of a man and a woman in lust unsanctified and uncreative. It may chance that, learning wisdom, this man and this woman exchange rings, and so turn lust into love, and enter kindly (with children growing about them) a slow winter of wisdom and withering. But if not, they are bound upon a wheel of torment that will carry them down into uttermost burning depths.

Magnus stood on the shore.

His mouth touched the sweet shivering mouth of the girl from the north. All around them the faces smiled. Erlend and Thora smiled. Hold Ragnarson winked lewdly. The bishop said that the wedding of Magnus and Ingerth would be celebrated immediately after Easter. Ingerth was taken by an old woman and a girl up to her chamber.

After the marriage, after the giving of rings, after the feast of harps and honey and wine, Magnus stood in the marriage chamber. Hold Ragnarson unthonged a shoe, and laughed, and nudged Magnus in the ribs, and went away into the darkness. The bride was brought by dimpling women to his door. The flame was in her. It wavered in her hands and breast and mouth. But from Magnus came no answering flame to mingle with hers. Now, at the moment of supreme earthly felicity, the fires that had tormented him were out.

Magnus looked at Ingerth hopelessly. He shook his head. The bed lay between them white and unbroken.

Magnus slept in his own room. He dreamed. He was in a place of burnings and ice. 'No,' said the voice of the friend beyond a fold of green wavering fire, 'but there is love indeed, and God ordained it, and it is a good love and necessary for the world's weal, and worthy are those who taste of it. But there are souls which cannot eat at that feast, for they serve another and a greater love, which is to these flames and meltings (wherein you suffer) the hard immortal diamond. Magnus, I call thee yet once more to the marriage feast of the king.' . . . Magnus opened his eyes. He lay in his own room in the great Hall; but he that called himself 'the keeper of the loom' had vanished.

From that hour – it is said – Magnus enrolled himself in the company of the virgins.

Yet for the sake of state and of policy and of the high position into which he had been born, Magnus lived in the great Hall with Ingerth his bride.

And the fire that had long tormented the bridegroom began to harden to a cold precious flame.

Fire and fire burned in their different intensities.

The women saw, after a week, how it was with Ingerth. She was like a bee imprisoned in a burning window. Magnus saw it too. He wept for the bitter ordinances of time.

The bride stood often on the cliff looking over the sea northwards.

Subtle witherings began to appear in her flesh before the summer was over.

Yet they lived in the same house and grew in time to have a tender regard one for another.

Hold Ragnarson, checking his laughter, looked bewildered from one face to the other.

That winter Ingerth sat at her loom in the great chamber and made a heavy winter coat for her husband (the equinox was past, and the north wind was putting the first black gurls on the sea beyond Birsay).

Magnus came up from the beach carrying a great halibut on his back. He had been fishing with Hold and Sigurd all morning.

Ingerth turned on him then eyes of longing and peace and love.

To Hold Ragnarson, since he continued to be perplexed at the cold marriage, Magnus one evening when they were alone together at the shore tried to explain – as best he could, and with many silences and hesitancies – what had happened.

'How shall I put it, my dear friend? It isn't that the rage of fire – which you so shrewdly observed in me in March and April – had died down. No, it is fiercer than ever. But it is no longer fixed on one object – the fertile conduit in the sweet flesh of woman – it has undergone a transmutation, it is diffused in a new feeling, a special regard for everyone who walks the earth, as if they all (even the tinkers on the road) were lords and princes. And this regard – it extends beyond human beings to the animals, it longs to embrace even water and stone. This summer I began to handle sea, shells, larks' eggs, a piece of cloth from the loom, with a delight I have never known before, not even as a child. You remember that morning last week when we fished with five Birsay men off Marwick Head. I had the helm myself. You remember that great lithe cod that was drawn in on the hook. Mans from Revay caught it. I was pierced with the beauty and the agony of the creature. But when I saw the practical hands of the fishermen setting to work at once with the knife, I knew that of course such cruelty is needful in the world. Pain is woven through and through the stuff of life. Ingerth is suffering now, because of me. I suffer too, because of Ingerth and everyone I have had dealings with. Is God to blame for all this suffering? What an empty question! Look at the agony on this crucifix I have round my neck. This crucifix is the forge, and the threshing-floor, and the shed of the net-makers, where God and man work out together a plan of utter necessity and of unimaginable beauty . . .'

Hold Ragnarson smiled at the deep sincerity of his friend – expressed in falterings and sudden fluencies – and at the beauty of the images he uttered, as they walked together along the cliff verges of Marwick that sunset. He smiled with simulated understanding, but in truth he was more perplexed than ever.

The stretching and sheeting and shrouding. Silence. A summons then for great ones to hasten to Trondheim on urgent horses. East from Scotland under a black sail came Magnus Erlendson; and solemn faces came about him on the shore when the sail was furled in the fiord and the small boat was drawn up. Through high dark narrow streets Magnus was led by foreign voices to the great kirk that was there, a God-steading, the high cathedral of Norway. Inside it was as cold and green and silent as the heart of an iceberg. Two candles, four vigilant sword-gleams, defined the catafalque. Then Magnus came to the source of silence, to the folded hands and still face of Erlend Thorfinnson, earl of Orkney, lord of Shetland and Caithness and Lewis (a far-farer now to ghostly feast-halls); and he kissed the coldness, and a candle-flame wavered, and Magnus said, 'Take thy coat of peace about thee, old father, and go forward.' Later, after he had wept, he said, 'Comfort me now, kind one, keeper of the loom.' Then in a silence deeper than silence the dark weave of voices, the threnody, *Requiem aeternam da ei, Domine.*

A many a voice about him then, on quayside and garden and curtained chamber. Their consolation bothered Magnus like summer insects. 'A great sorrow indeed is fallen on Orkney . . .' 'It happens to all men, high and low . . .' 'The whole of Scandinavia mourns . . .' 'Look, Magnus, the sailors have black bands in their caps . . .' 'My son, he has gone to the repose of Paradise . . .' 'The king sends deepest commiseration. The king is much occupied with affairs of state in Bergen. The king has ordered court mourning for seven days. The king will of course see you before you leave for Orkney. Meantime, my lord – if it is convenient for you – Aristius desires your presence in the chancellery, after the funeral . . .'

The dead one was thrust down into a mine of perdurable light, and sealed with marble and with lead.

A lift and stir of white beard, the touch of old-mouth wetness to Magnus's cheek, sour-buttermilk breath, a few bleak elegiac words, then this: 'Permit me, my lord, if you would be so kind, there is something I am longing to show you, this way, the wardrobe is over here, permit an old man to show you a certain worthy thing, one of particular interest to you. But first, my lord, as to your dear dead father – the lord Erlend Thorfinnson was good enough to repose in me a certain measure of trust, you understand, I standing as it were close to the throne in my office as chancellor, and so I hope, my lord, that I may expect the like trust and confidence from you, also, in time . . . The king will see you in due course. He is up to his eyes in business. He is as you know young: he stands much in need of vigilance and counsel . . . How this key squeals! . . . Here then, here it is, look now, such magnificence, the coat-of-state of the earls of Orkney, isn't it a fine piece of workmanship, Gilborne wove it in his shop in Paris seventy-eight years ago, feel how heavy it is, look at that embroidery on the collar, exquisite. Touch it, lord Magnus, it's yours after all, it belongs to you, you are to take it west to Orkney (as soon as the king gives permission for the ship to leave). Or rather, the coat belongs both to you and to your cousin Earl Hakon Paulson. This is – I admit – a situation of some delicacy and difficulty. The coat can hardly be sliced in two with a sword, that would be worse than useless, besides of course it would be the ruination of an exquisite work of art. I thought however that you might wish to try it on, before I return it to the wardrobe. No? But . . . Very well . . . My lord, then, there are a few bits of preliminary business, you understand, things that will have to be attended to at once pertaining to your earldom in the west, a clearing of the ground. You will of course offer your allegiance to the King of Norway (I am to arrange your journey to Bergen as soon as may be convenient: ten days or a fortnight, perhaps). If you will be kind enough to step over here to the table at the window. I have written down a few items.' . . .

Creak of parchment. Old crafty squinnying eyes. Old parchment mouth moving.

'VIKINGS – There are nests of those so-called sea adventurers all along the coast from Barra to Unst: a constant threat to peace, property, security. They must be smoked out. It will be advisable to act in co-operation with Earl Hakon Paulson.'

'I agree to that,' said Magnus.

'AGRICULTURE AND FISHING – Ancient custom and usage to be maintained. That is, the peasant to be subject to laird, earl, church, and king: these have a just claim on the first-fruits of his labour, whether corn or fish, offering him in return the strong shield of law. The peasant will pay the rent fixed by his lord. The peasant will take arms when called on in defence of his lord. He will let his lord look first upon the whiteness of his daughters before they go to their husbands.'

'Shameless. Foul.'

'VAGRANTS – All tinkers, hawkers, pedlars, beggars to be moved on wherever found, and scourged if necessary; and so sent on.

'ROADS AND FERRIES – The existing tolls and charges—'

Magnus said, 'That's enough for one day. Aristius, I'm tired. Men make too much of death, in the wrong way. I agree about the Vikings. God's poor are not to be molested – tinkers are immortal spirits under their rags . . .

'Aristius, I am anxious to get home as soon as possible. Tell the king that. I can't bide here indefinitely. There are many things I must discuss in Orkney with Earl Hakon Paulson. I have arranged the voyage with my skipper, Thorkel Swart. The *Selkie* is to sail on Friday morning. If you can arrange an audience with the king before I leave, good and well.'

A hoisting of silvery eyebrows, silence, writhen fingers on a pliant elbow; then a mysterious slow freighted whisper: 'My lord, the king bids me say this. The king, though he has not yet met you, has formed the highest regard for your character. The king desires his islands in the west to be ruled by a loyal strong earl. There are not lacking ways and means whereby in the course of a few years Magnus Erlendson might be the sole earl in Orkney. On his shoulders alone will hang the coat-of-earldom.'

'The coat belongs equally to Earl Hakon and me,' said Magnus.

Magnus was glad to be out and away at last from the whisperings and arras-stirrings and duplicities of statecraft. He had been bidden farewell at the palace door by a somewhat cold and hurt councillor Aristius (whose last words had been that the king would take it ill if Magnus sailed for Orkney, as he said he intended to do, without the royal leave and blessing). He walked down a narrow street, at the end of which were booths for the sale of dried fish, ivory, oil, cloth, butter and cheese, and emerged on to the waterfront. Out in the fiord the *Selkie* rode at anchor with furled sail. And there, at the harbour steps, stood Thorkel Swart the skipper.

'Thorkel,' shouted Magnus happily, 'we're bound home on Friday.'

Thorkel said gloomily that two of the sailors were missing since the night before. Thring had seen them in an ale-house. They had gone on from there no doubt to some brothel or stew. He supposed they might turn up in the morning with hangovers and, possibly, poxes.

The old man smiled at Magnus out of black broken teeth. He loosed the rope from the bollard and followed Magnus down the seven harbour steps.

'Did you order a web of cloth?' said Thorkel.

The small boat rocked under them. Thorkel fitted an oar into a rowlock.

'Did I? I may have done,' said Magnus.

'A man spoke to me at the harbour,' said Thorkel. 'A young man. He said he had some business with you. He bade me to tell you that the work on the cloth was going along fine. "A fold of light." That's the way he put it. He said he would see you about it sometime. But if we sail on Friday . . .'

Magnus trailed fingers in the cold water.

'I'm worried about Ragnar and Sven,' said Thorkel Swart. 'One of my men was found in this same harbour with his throat cut. That was six years ago. I remember it well.'

The oars made small musical circles in the water.

Earl Magnus's private chapel at Paplay in Orkney. A monk enters, from the monastery in Eynhallow.

TEMPTER: Magnus, I see you're at your prayers. I hope in God's name I don't interrupt you. I've come from Father Abbot in Eynhallow with an urgent message for you – a summons – an entreaty.

MAGNUS: What does Father Abbot want?

TEMPTER: My lord, the way Father Abbot sees it is this. You've been earls in Orkney now, yourself and Hakon Paulson, for five years – and things have hardly gone well, have they?

To be brutal, things could hardly be worse.

It's the old sorry tale – two earls, one small domain, a sundered allegiance. There was bound to be trouble. There always was in the past, in a like situation.

MAGNUS: Things weren't always like this. At the beginning Hakon and I did things well together. We destroyed the Vikings – in Shetland we smoked them out like wasps. We made good laws and set our two seals on the parchment. Everybody knew they were good laws. There was prosperity too. The merchants built ships. There was bread and fish for the poor. Loom and harp were busy in every island.

TEMPTER: My lord, what went wrong? There's curses, blood, black eyes whenever Magnus's men meet Hakon's men in the ale-house.

You and Hakon never meet now. You sulk in opposite corners of Orkney.

There may be worse to come – civil war, mercenaries riding through the cornfields. Murder. Burning. Rape.

You have lost control of the situation.

Father Abbot wishes me to say this to you. All winter the monasteries have been praying and it seems that now God has given us the perfect answer. It is this, that you become one of us in Eynhallow. There's a cell ready for you. We will receive you with all reverence and charity. There you can bide in peace all the rest of your days. We even have a name for you: Brother Pax.

MAGNUS: No.

TEMPTER: Study sanctity, my lord. Pray for your people. Prepare your soul for heaven.

MAGNUS: No.

TEMPTER: Orkney must have a single earl. That is the only cure for our troubles. Hakon is stronger than you.

Come with me now, pilgrim.

I have a boat ready on the beach outside.

MAGNUS: No. Tell the abbot it is not right for a coward to wear the long bright holy coat. God has made me an earl in this place. The harp is bleeding, I know it. My work is a work of peace, to bind up the wounds in the music. I must learn to harp well among the seven red beasts.

TEMPTER: The boatman is waiting. The tide is just exactly right.

MAGNUS: (*shouting*) No. Leave me.

TEMPTER: My lord, it may interest you to know this. Barns in Hamnavoe were set on fire last night. Foreign horsemen have been seen in Scorradale. One of your ships was sunk in Scapa this morning. This harp of yours – swords have smashed it to pieces already. Earl Hakon has broken through. It is war.

MAGNUS: Thank you for your news. There is a sword in the porch. Bring it to me, please.

TEMPTER: Wouldn't your lordship be better with a psalter? Remember the battle in Menai. We monks still laugh when we remember that.

MAGNUS: My sword.

TEMPTER: Well then, it seems I must row back alone.

(*He gives Magnus the sword.*)

MAGNUS: Tell Father Abbot I'll see him when the war is over.

(*The Tempter goes out. Earl Magnus offers his sword at the altar. The Keeper-of-the-Loom stands at his shoulder.*)

KEEPER OF LOOM: What are you doing, pilgrim, with that sharp thing in your fist? Those who take the sword shall perish by the sword. That sword will cut your heavenly weave to shreds. Only a child or an angel could endure such shining. Snow sunlight would filthy it . . . Go out on the roads with that sword, Magnus, and you'll lose everything.

(*Magnus turns from the Keeper-of-the-Loom. He takes his sword out into the sunlight.*)

KEEPER OF LOOM: And yet there is no other way. He must go.

Far on, Magnus came to a place of burnt and broken stone, in the darkness of night, alone.

Scarecrow

All one spring and summer troops of horsemen rode through the district, this way and that. Mans would hear the clatter of hooves in the darkness of early morning going past the end of his house. He would lie beside the quiet-breathing Hild, shaking with terror. The horsemen rode on then over the shoulder of the hill. Mans made a thick bar for the door out of the piece of ship's mast he had once found on the shore. But that, he knew, would never keep them out.

The peasants of Revay sowed the barley seed in their furrows one morning. They had hardly finished when they saw a troop against the skyline. They left their seed baskets among the furrows and ran inside. But the horsemen rode on in the direction of Hundland.

War had broken out between the two earls, Hakon Paulson and Magnus Erlendson. The large farmers adhered to this faction or that – whichever seemed most advantageous to them – and they expected their tenants to follow their lead. The peasants had no idea what it was all about. All they knew was that life had suddenly become very unpleasant for them. The horsemen of Earl Hakon would ride into the district one morning. They would ask the peasants to provide them with butter and cheese and bread. When the troubles were over, they said, of course Earl Hakon would settle up with them. He would pay them generously. The peasants had heard that kind of talk before; or if they had not heard it their fathers and their grandfathers had heard it; and the cruelty and destructiveness of the horsemen were a part of their lore. They always kept a little aside, of course, for the horsemen: some rounds of hard white cheese, a jar or two of sour butter, a tough old hen or two. They knew that otherwise the horsemen would ransack their barns and sties and cupboards with cold hands, and ride away leaving a bare wounded district behind them.

There would be peace for a day or two. Then, some evening when the men of Revay would be talking in Prem the weaver's, or in the smithy, they would hear a disordered clatter of hooves over the cobbles. Men with black patches on their tunics: this time it was a band of Earl Magnus Erlendson's men. They were tired, they had ridden far, they had been holding the Dounby crossroads all day against those bandits of the usurper Hakon Paulson. Therefore (said the leader with a kind of false heartiness that filled Mans and the other peasants with as much fear as the cold rapacity of the others) they would consider it a favour if they could spend the night in the district. No, they didn't want anything to eat, they had eaten well enough at Twatt and Isbister as they passed through. They would be no trouble at all, the leader assured the Revay men of that. All they wanted to do was rest. However, if the people insisted on entertaining them for a few hours, the horsemen would like that very much – a dance, perhaps, a sing-song, a chance to talk to a girl or two. The leader winked at the men of Revay. The horsemen laughed all around him. Soldiering for the true earl, Earl Magnus Erlendson, was a hard business. The horsemen needed a bit of relaxation now and then. That big barn over there beside the standing stone – that looked a good place for a dance. Yes, indeed, the horsemen would be glad to accept the peasants' hospitality . . . So, the women and the girls had to be rounded up from their butter-making and ale-churning and cradle-rocking and herded into the big barn beside the water. And Skop the piper, sick at heart, had to sit in a corner of the barn all night making skirls and rants. And – it was like an evil dream –

the peasants saw their wives and sweethearts and daughters being taken out under the stars from time to time by this trooper and that . . . At daybreak the horsemen would ride away again.

Clatter of hooves on the road, thud of hooves on the hillside. Peasants all over Orkney and Shetland quaked with terror when they heard that sound. Even a distant sight of the horsemen was enough. There one stood at the Birsay shore, looking out to sea. A dozen silhouettes went in order over the shoulder of Greenay hill. That was enough. The peasants dropped whatever they were doing. They ran inside and drew the bars across the doors (not that that would be much help, if the horsemen thought of paying a call).

These mercenaries were evil, whatever side they supported. Mans knew a few of these men; they had been peasants like himself; they had sailed in the *Sea Eagle* to Anglesey and Scilly; one or two had even toiled beside him at the rowing bench. They had come to like this free rootless life, and, when the war in the west was over, had never returned to the hard strict cycle of work on the land. But most of the horsemen that year were strangers – Irishmen, Hebrideans, Swedes. They were professional soldiers who hired themselves to whatever king or robber chief or Viking paid best. Earl Magnus or Earl Hakon – it was all one to them. Let them see the shine of the silver in their hands, and then they put their daggers to the grindstone. Some of them had been as far as Byzantium and Novgorod, following their trade of war. They had great stories to tell, once they were flushed with ale over the croft fires: even Mans had to admit that. And they could sing ballads and shanties in French or Gaelic or English. It was as if, having no ties of family or nation, they belonged to a great brotherhood. When one of them said something lewd or witty, a wild free gust of merriment went through them, very different from the gentle half-reluctant mirth of Mans and the other peasants (as if laughter was a very uncertain spring in a barren world). But when it came to business, all the joviality was wiped from the faces of these men. Then the peasants saw the hard cruel bone underneath.

There were rumours of how far they would go, those horse-men, if they were put to it. Jock and Mary the tinkers passed through Revay once a month at least with stories from this parish and that. A troop of horsemen (they said) had called at the farm of a man in Orphir called Glum. They had asked Glum to sell them a side of bacon. Glum would be paid by the true earl once the troubles were over. Glum had answered that he had no bacon, as he did not keep pigs on his farm. The leading horseman said they were going to the burn to water their horses, and they expected Glum to have the flitch of bacon ready for them when they came back. Glum shrugged his shoulders. Glum's wife ran distractedly among the crofts, asking somebody for God's sake to lend Glum a piece of bacon at least. The horsemen returned. Glum stood in his door and shook his head at them. He would love to oblige the soldiers. He was sorry, but he had had no luck with the rearing of pigs. The horsemen dismounted. One of them took the halter from his horse. The others laid hold on Glum and they dragged him into his barn and they hanged him from a rafter. Glum's wife stood in the door screaming. She had gotten the loan of a smoked haunch of pork from the priest down at the shore and she still clutched it and howled as Glum her good-man kicked and shrugged himself to death, half way between the rafter and the barn floor. The horsemen got tired of the noise of Glum's wife. They locked her in the byre beside the cow. Later they searched the farm, but what Glum had told them was true, there were no pig-sties.

These horsemen, said the tinkers, were mercenaries of Earl Hakon.

But the mercenaries of Earl Magnus, said the tinkers, had done something even worse in the parish of Firth. There was a

farmer in the hills of Firth called Aud. Aud was a very good
kind-hearted man, said the tinkers (and they should know). He
had a wife called Sig and a daughter called Frey. One morning
Aud saw a troop of horsemen riding through the hills between
Harray and Rendall, two miles away. The horsemen turned in
the direction of Aud's farm. Aud set his wife and daughter on
ponies and told them to ride to his brother's farm in Stenness
until the horsemen had taken whatever they wanted and passed
on. Aud went to the boundary of his land and greeted the
horsemen. He saw at once that they had been in some kind of a
skirmish. One or two had blood on their hands and beards, and
the leader had a filthy bandage round his neck. 'We understand,' said this man, 'that you have a good-looking wife and a
young daughter on your farm.' Aud said that unfortunately he
was a bachelor. He wished it was true that he had a wife and a
daughter. He had proposed marriage to one or two girls in his
time, but either they or their fathers had turned him down. He
had never been what you would call good-looking, with that big
wart on the side of his nose and his squint teeth. That, he
supposed, was why the girls had never taken to him. Also of
course it was a poor kind of a hill farm he kept here in Firth. Oh
no, he was just a lonely old farmer, and all he prayed for now
was to end his days in peace . . . Aud was a sharp-witted man.
He saw at once that the horsemen were of the Magnus faction,
because of the black patches on their sleeves. 'So the sooner the
good Earl Magnus wins this war,' he said, 'the better for us all.
One thing sure, Earl Magnus has the bravest and best soldiers in
the world.' . . . The horseman said, 'I think the farmer is trying
to make a fool of us.' Then Aud knew that they were resentful
because they had been beaten in the skirmish. 'We fought well,'
said the leader. 'We did our best. We can't always be winning.
They ambushed us. Now we would welcome the company of a
woman or two.' . . . Aud said that there were no women at the
farm. 'Search the house,' he said. The horsemen dismounted.

Aud remarked that it was good weather for the time of year. He
hoped the sergeant's neck would soon heal – that was a nasty
wound he had got. The horsemen returned to say that they had
searched the farm and the out-houses and all they could find in
the way of women was one old hag washing clothes in a pool at
the back of the house. 'We will go and see her,' said the leader.
Aud said that the washerwoman was old Brunn, his servant. She
was over ninety years old. 'The farmer will come with us too,'
said the leader. They forced Aud to go with them to the back of
the house. It was true enough, an old woman with a sunken face
and whiskers about her mouth was scrubbing shirts and
drawers in a pool. The pool was fed by a small hidden tinkling
burn from the hill. The old woman finished her washing and
began to spread the clothes on the grass. 'She is too old,' said the
leader. Brunn looked at Aud standing among the horsemen and
said, 'I see you have guests, Aud. What a pity you sent Sig and
Frey away this morning. You will not be able to entertain them
by yourself. I am too old for setting tables.' . . . 'What will we do
with this liar?' said the leader. 'Wash his tongue,' said a man
with a bandage on his wrist – 'wash the lies out of his mouth.'
They tied Aud's hands behind him with a bit of rope. 'Queer
guests,' said old Brunn. Aud said it was true enough he had sent
his wife and daughter to Stenness that morning, as soon as he
had seen the horsemen coming. He said he was very glad he had
done so. His wife and daughter were the most beautiful women
in Orkney. The horsemen threw Aud into the pool. He made a
great splash before he sank. 'Tut-tut,' said the old washer-
woman, 'what a way to carry on, Aud.' Aud's head rose out of
the water and he said, 'I am very glad that you were beaten in
the skirmish. You must be poor soldiers.' One of the horsemen
picked up a large stone. 'Tut,' said old Brunn, 'you're getting
your clothes washed today, Aud, without taking them off.' The
horseman threw the stone at Aud's brimming head. 'God
forgive us all,' said Aud. The stone struck him. He sank and

did not rise again. Old Brunn said to the soldiers in her faded voice, 'I put the curse of trows on you. I put on you the curse of harelips. I put on you the cough curse and the curse of the knotted haunch. I put on you the four curses of wind and earth and water and fire. I put these curses on you because you have killed Aud who was a good and a generous man.' . . . The horsemen laughed. They turned their horses' heads and re-mounted and rode out of the farmstead. Old Brunn wrung out the last gray stocking and stretched it on the grass beside the woollen shirt.

The tinkers went on to say that they had been in the island of Stronsay ten days previously. In Stronsay some horsemen had called at the smithy. The blacksmith there was a man called Nord. He was immensely strong. He was rather disliked by some of the islanders because he had a forthright way of speaking. Nord was making an iron grill for the Hall of Stronsay when the horsemen rode into his yard. Nord saw at once that they were Earl Hakon's men, because they had red patches sewn on their sleeves. He didn't bother to greet them. The horsemen stood for a while against the wall while Nord brought the white-hot iron from the forge to the anvil. Then for a minute or two there was a terrible clangour and din, as Nord struck at the graying iron with his hammer. The blacksmith's upper body was naked, and it shone with sweat. Not till Nord had plunged the iron into cold water and the last hissings had died away did he turn to the horsemen and say, 'Are you wanting something?' 'Yes,' said the lieutenant, 'we have a dozen horses outside and we would like you to shoe them.' Nord said that he had no time that day. He was making a grill for the laird's kitchen and there was still a certain amount of work to be done on it. 'However,' said the leader of the horsemen, 'our horses require shoes urgently. We have to be in Sanday before nightfall, and we have been told there is no blacksmith in that island.' Nord con-sidered for a while. He put his foot up on the anvil and his

elbow on his knee and he fingered his beard. Then he said he
was prepared to shoe all the horses, but only on condition that
he was well paid for the job. 'You will be well paid,' said the
officer. Nord said that he required the money in advance. The
lieutenant said, 'Unfortunately that is not possible. You will be
paid in full once Earl Hakon Paulson has crushed the rebellion.'
Nord laughed. He bade the horsemen good-day. The laird was a
good patron of his and he paid on the nail. He had wasted too
much time speaking. Now he must hurry and finish the grill
before sunset. The leader ordered one of his men to bring the
first of the horses into the smithy. Nord went on working at the
grill as if horse and horsemen did not exist. He put a bar of iron
in the forge. The leader said to Nord that the first horse was
waiting to be shod. Nord snatched the iron out of glare and held
it under the horse's head. The horse screamed and reared and
flung his hooves all over the smithy. The horsemen turned on
Nord then and seized him. Several of them were burnt by the
iron bar before they bore him to the floor and put ropes round
him. Twelve horsemen fought in the smithy that day to secure
Nord the blacksmith. 'What should we do with this blacksmith?' said the leader. 'I think we should cool him in his bucket
of water,' said a horseman with sword scars on his face. Another
– this one had got burnt on the wrist – said, 'I think we should
open his head with an axe to see what makes a man so stupid.'
The leader said that they would make a present to the laird that
day of a roasted ox. They put the almost-finished grill into the
forge till it was red-hot. They brought it out then and set it on
the floor. Then they tied Nord down on it. 'Roar, ox,' said the
leader. Nord did not say a thing, though his eyes bulged. 'We
must cook you well, you are such a big ox,' said a horseman.
And another said, 'They will be pleased with their new grill in
the Hall of Stronsay tonight, and the meat on it.' It was
fortunate for Nord that just then there were shouts at the
end of the village, and a clatter of hooves. The laird of Stronsay

was a supporter of Earl Magnus Erlendson. He had been told
that some of Earl Hakon's mercenaries were in the island, and
he had ridden to meet them with a strong force of servants and
retainers. Earl Hakon's horsemen left the smithy at once. At the
door the leader turned and said to the iron-fast figure on the
floor, 'Nord, we will come back another day for the horse
shoes.' The troop galloped away towards the far end of the
island. The people of Stronsay said that if Nord had not been
such a strong man that torture would certainly have killed him.
As things turned out he was back at work in three days, but he
would go to his grave with that checker-work of burnings on his
body. 'I enjoy my ale much better now,' said Nord – 'that grill
put a dryness on me. I did not make horse shoes for the
murderers either.' Some of the islanders said that Nord de-
served the pain he had suffered, because of his stupidity and
arrogance.

These were some of the stories that Jock and Mary the tinkers
told the people of Revay that spring. Old Mary did most of the
talking. She had a vivid tongue. Mans heard the sizzle of flesh
under the branding iron, and the last watery breath of the
drowning man. Hild, listening quietly in the corner, grew cold
as stone.

Then the tinkers went away, and the peasants returned to
their labour in the fields.

A week went past.

One morning Hild said, 'Mans, do you know this, I think the
war might be over.'

Mans said nothing.

'There hasn't been a horseman in this parish for ten days,'
said Hild. 'Earl Hakon and Earl Magnus have made a treaty at
last – I'm sure of it.'

'I would hold my tongue,' said Mans. 'What do women know
about these things?'

That same morning Fergus, a monk, walked across from the

church on the island. A boy went before Fergus and rang a bell. They came solemnly and silently over the fields. Mans and Hild knew why the monk had come to Revay. Old Trev who worked a croft on the other side of the hill had been sick for a week. He was said to be over eighty years old. The church was taking to the dying man last oil and viaticum.

Right towards Mans' door came the boy with the tinkling bell and the monk with the consecrated Host. Mans called out to him, 'Fergus, they say Magnus and Hakon have signed a peace. Is that true?'

Boy and monk paid no more attention than if Mans had been a sheep bleating.

They walked on trance-like past the door.

Hild crossed herself as the Blessed Sacrament went by.

An hour later monk and boy returned. Fergus carried the empty pyx and the bell and the boy was bending down and plucking primroses here and there.

The boy laughed in the sunlight.

They came to the end of Mans' house, where Mans and Hild were forking dung out of a manure heap.

Mans put on a sad face and said, 'How is he, old Trev?'

'He has gone to God in peace,' said Fergus, smiling.

Hild crossed herself again.

'Well now,' said Mans, 'they say the war is over. I heard in the smithy that the earls have signed a treaty.'

'I know nothing about that,' said Fergus.

'It's true,' said Mans. 'The soldiers are disbanded. They've been paid their bounty. They've gone away to Ireland, to the wars there. There's not a horseman left in Orkney.'

'I think old Trev is the only happy one,' said Fergus solemnly. 'Many a peasant will be wishing for his kind of peace before this summer is over.'

The boy and the monk passed on. The boy said he knew where there was a lark's nest. Fergus said he was not to touch the eggs. He was to run along to the mill and ask the miller to deliver five sacks of meal to the bakehouse on the Brough. There was likely to be a shortage of meal before the end of the summer. The very poor and the sick depended on the monastery for their bread. A small amount of meal was required also to ensure a continuing supply of sacramental hosts. He had heard that a huge troop of horsemen had been seen at Yesnaby that same morning.

Fergus and the boy passed out of Mans' hearing. He saw the boy run down through the fields towards the mill.

'I doubt the war is not over yet,' said Hild.

Six more days passed, and still there was not a horseman to be seen.

Mans and the other peasants of Revay slung their seed baskets over their shoulders. They strode about the side of the hill, ritually, from morning to nightfall. The golden rain slashed from their fists.

Another week went past.

Mans made a scarecrow at the end of his cottage of two bits of driftwood and some sacking.

Hild's black hen went missing that same morning. 'That black hen,' she said, 'I've had no eggs from her for a month. I'm sure she's laying among the heather. I'll go and look for her once I get this cheese made.'

When Mans came to his corn rig carrying the scarecrow he saw Hild on the slope above. She was searching here and there among the heather. She probed and poked among the tough springy meshes. It was a beautiful morning in early summer. The sun glittered out of loch and the wind went in fluent undulations among the tall grass. The first faint flush of green had gone over the ploughlands of Birsay. Mans' scarecrow stood in the centre of his rig. It creaked in the wind and fluttered its rags. The monks uttered plainchant under a distant arch.

'There's not much chance of finding an egg in all that heather,' shouted Mans.

Hild uttered low sweet cajolery here and there. 'Mag Midnight. The pretty black girl. Come to Hild, then. Chooky chook. Blackness. The sweetheart. The jewel.'

Now that the seed was uttered upon the land the peasants waited for the sun and the rain to do their bit. What they had performed was an act of faith. They trusted that the seed they had buried would return from the grave, first the shoot, then the ear, then the stalk with a full burden of corn in the ear. But this yearly resurrection of the seed was encompassed with dangers. The rain might fall in black deluges on the hill all the month of June. The sun might shrivel the crop with unwonted ardency while it was still green. More terrible still, the black worm might bore into the root.

The peasants had done what they could. They had spread the dung and seaweed carefully on the black fields. The bishop had come and blessed the tilth. So far the weather had been good. Showers of rain fell, mainly during the night. The sun shone plentifully as the days got longer. The seed, sown in faith, had so far been well nourished and warmed.

Hild drew back a tuft of heather and found three eggs among the roots and the gray stones. She cried out with joy. She put them carefully in her sackcloth apron.

Also next winter's fire had been dug out of the hill. All the previous week Mans and Hild had been up among the peatcuttings with the other crofters. First they had sliced the fleece of heather off, and then they had sunk their tuskers into the steep banks of squelching bog. Up came the black squares, and the women had spread them in thousands to dry all about the cuttings, while the dogs barked below and the larks sang above and small black insistent flies tormented their breathing. The sun had stored that fire in the earth for them, ages ago. It only needed the kiss of flint, some cold morning next winter, for the peats to chortle and send out flowers of flame. 'It is a wonderful providence of God,' said the bishop.

'God makes sure that you have to sweat for it all the same,' said Mans to the other peasants in the ale-house.

Hild said a 'Hail Mary' to Our Lady of Fires.

The peasants had done everything to ensure that it would be a year of plenty in Birsay. They had tarred their boats to be ready for the haddock fishing. They had delivered the ewes in the last of the snow, and set small new flutters and bleats astray on the hillside. They had cleared the choked well of stones.

The bishop had made his crosses here and there: over the buried seed, over the boats, over the sheepfolds and the byres and the sties.

About a gross excess of sun or of rain the peasants could do little. Something had to be left to God. About the worm in the root they could do nothing. About the horsemen who had ranged here and there about Orkney all the previous winter and spring they could do less than nothing.

Three long shadows fell across the field. The horsemen had ridden along the ridge of the hill from the Isbister district, and the heather had deadened the hoof-falls. The three men wore red patches on their tunics.

The leading horseman said to Mans, 'Did a troop pass this way at first light?'

'What do I know about that?' said Mans. 'I was in bed then. I was asleep.'

The horsemen looked at him as if he was some kind of obdurate ox.

'What horsemen were you looking for?' said Hild quickly.

'Men with black patches,' said the leader. 'Bandits of the upstart Erlendson.'

'No,' said Mans, 'I saw no men with black patches.'

'We are no longer speaking to you, bedfart,' said the horseman. 'We are speaking to this henwife.'

'I heard horsemen on the loch-side road,' said Hild. 'I heard hooves a while back, when I was lighting the fire. That was in the early morning. They went that way.' . . . She pointed south towards Marwick and the cliffs of Sandwick.

The horsemen tugged at the reins and the horses reared and turned their heads towards the sea. The horsemen settled themselves in their saddles.

'We might get to the mill before them yet,' said the leader. He urged his gelding forward. The hooves whispered out of the long heather and thudded softly on over Mans' rig of young tender corn, and on past the scarecrow's impotent gesture.

Mans ran after them. 'That's my field,' he shouted. 'Don't you know a cornfield when you see it? You're worse than the wild pigs.'

'Be quiet, Mans,' murmured Hild at his shoulder.

'You're trampling on the bread of the people!' yelled Mans from the edge of his field.

The horsemen did not trouble to turn their heads. The hooves made scattered clops on the road below. A finger pointed. The troop rode in the direction of the mill.

Mans' eyes followed them out of sight. He was gray with fear and rage, and his fists trembled. 'Them and their wars,' he shouted. 'Hakon and Magnus, damn and blast the pair of them. Didn't we have enough bloody war the time the King of Norway came and took us away in his ship? Damn them all. Damn Magnus and Hakon and their bloody horsemen!'

He squatted down at the edge of the field. His eyes brooded over the tramplings that had just been made across the fecund green and black.

'We must just have patience,' said Hild. She sat down in the heather beside him, guarding the clutch of eggs (one warm) in her apron. 'They'll come to their senses soon. If they go on fighting like this the lairds will soon be as poor as the peasants. They'll stop it once their tapestries are in tatters. Just wait till their hawks are all wild.'

Mans' brief anger smouldered and went out. He plucked a blade of grass and nibbled it.

'Prem and me,' he said, 'we were speaking about it last night. I was up at Prem's, if you remember. Well, I did have a pint. I'll tell you what I said to Prem. He had set up his loom and was stretching a warp. "Prem," I said, "we're one folk. We all hang together, we're all of a piece. Priest, ploughman, laird, tinker, earl, we're all woven together in a kind of a coat. Now the coat's in tatters, and Orkney's naked," I said. "That's what war means in the end – everyone trying to cover himself from the east wind with his own bit of rag." . . . That's what I said to Prem. The loom put that picture in my mind.'

'That Mag Midnight lays a good egg,' said Hild.

'There was still a bit of bread last winter,' said Mans. 'There'll be none next winter. Just you wait. We'll be begging for crusts at the door of the monastery. Them bloody horsemen have eaten up everything.'

A voice said quietly behind them, 'What are you shouting about, eh?'

There were seven horsemen with black patches on their sleeves against the sky. The hooves whispered in the heather.

'I asked,' said the leader, 'what you were making all the noise about?'

'Nothing,' mumbled Mans.

The horsemen looked at each other. One of them snickered.

Hild, looking back towards her house, saw that all the doors in the township were closed and the windows shuttered. The peasants of Revay had seen the horsemen coming a long way off.

'He seemed to be having a talk with his scarecrow,' said a young horseman. 'What did you have to say to your scarecrow, mister?'

Mans hung his head.

'I'll tell you what it is,' said Hild. 'My man had a drop too much ale in his porridge this morning.'

The horsemen laughed.

'Drunkard,' said the leader, 'did you see a troop of horsemen crossing this hill today?'

'I saw nothing,' said Mans. 'A peasant must mind his own business. All a peasant has time to see is his plough and his scythe and his flail.'

'There were horsemen on this hill an hour back,' said Hild. 'They had red patches on their sleeves. They rode south in the direction of Marwick. That's as sure as I'm standing here, sir.'

Two of the horsemen nodded and tugged at their bridles.

Another pointed down at the mill. The troop turned the heads of their horses.

'Thank God,' Hild whispered under her breath.

'Wait a minute,' said the leader. 'What's that you've got in your lap, woman?'

'It's nothing,' said Mans.

'I wasn't speaking to you, tosspot,' said the leader, still looking at Hild.

'It's a couple of eggs, sir,' said Hild. 'My old black hen, she comes and she lays eggs in the heather here.'

'The captain is hungry,' said the young horseman. 'He had no breakfast this morning.'

'I'm going to clip her wings, that's what I'm going to do,' said Hild. 'She'll bide round the door then.'

'So what about the captain's breakfast, eh?' said the young horseman, holding out his palm.

'The bishop will hear about this,' muttered Mans.

The young soldier dismounted. He took a dagger from his belt. He strolled over towards Mans. 'Did the drunkard say something?' he said. 'I thought the drunkard made some remark.'

'No, it's all right,' said Hild. 'Here, you're welcome to the eggs.'

'We'll be coming back this way soon,' said the leader. 'We'll call in for a drop of that marvellous ale of yours, ma'am, that can make a man drunk and brave first thing in the morning.'

The troop hesitated at the edge of the ploughed land.

'I think,' said one of the horsemen, 'we'd better go round by the hill. Earl Magnus put out that order, remember: the cornfields are not to be trampled.'

'Never mind that,' said the leader. 'Our job now is to rout them out of the mill.' He urged his horse on over the young corn. The other horsemen followed. One of them, a tall Icelander, began to sing. They all raised their heads and shouted a chorus.

> I wish I was far from here
> I wish I was home in bed
> Pretty Ragn in my arms
> A jug of ale at my head

One of them threw the scarecrow down as he went past. They were still singing when they reached the road and spurred their horses on southward.

Hild looked furtively at Mans. She saw that there were tears of shame in his eyes. There was silence between them for a while, then he began to vent his rage and humiliation on Hild. 'You had no right,' he shouted, 'to tell them I was drunk. That's a lie. I'm not drunk. There's not enough malt left in Revay to make a mouse drunk.'

'I had to tell them something,' said Hild. 'I thought of Glum and Aud. I didn't want to be a widow before bedtime.'

Mans wandered into the middle of his rig, examining the trampled tillage. There were hoof-holes here and there in the green corn like the pocks of some disease. Hild murmured here and there about the hillside, searching for her black hen. The other Revay peasants were still barricaded inside their houses, in case the horsemen should decide to return. (The horsemen were like that, full of sudden whims and unpredictable notions; not like the peasants who were bound to the slow inexorable rituals of agriculture.)

Mans was offended with Hild. A wife should not tell lies about her husband. Drunkard indeed – he had been sober as a lawman for a month and more. But he had to speak to something, to relieve his feelings. He raised the fallen scarecrow. He drove the stave into the earth; he rooted it once more in the centre of his rig. 'Mister scarecrow,' he said, 'is that better then? How is it with you now? There you've been standing all day frightening the rooks. Listen, mister. I want to put in a word for them black birds. It isn't much they take, is it, a seed here and a grain there? . . . Why shouldn't I have a word with my own scarecrow, if I want to? What's so funny about that? . . . I was *not* drunk,' he shouted back to Hild . . . 'Well then,' he continued in a neighbourly voice to the scarecrow, 'what were we talking about? The rooks. I know it's your job to frighten them. But let me tell you one thing, mister. The rooks don't do all that much harm. No. It's them six-legged things made in God's image, the horsemen, it's them that I hate. They rape and they rob wherever the fancy takes them . . . Drunk, indeed! – no wife should tell lies about her man . . . I doubt you and I can do nothing about the horsemen, mister.'

'Mans,' Hild called urgently from the edge of the field.

'Shut your face,' said Mans. 'Shut your face. Telling lies about me to that scum. I was *not* drunk.'

'Mans,' she called, 'there's more horsemen.'

There were shouts from further up the hill.

Mans stood earth-rooted like his own scarecrow. He looked neither right nor left. It would be fatal to run. The horsemen loved nothing better than to stick their lances into fleeing stumbling backsides. He gave one swift glance from under his brows at Hild. She had the black hen in her arms and was walking slowly in the direction of the cottage. He turned and followed her, walking like a man who is going home a little tranced and weary from his day's work. He looked neither up the hill nor down the hill. His feet rose and fell in the heather.

It seemed unlikely that he would get home before the order came for him to stop. Hild and he arrived at the threshold at the same time (he had longer legs than his wife). Once there, Mans took Hild by the shoulder and hurled her in through the door. The black hen made a wild squawking in the gloom. They were all inside then. Mans shut the door and threw the bar across it. The black hen fluttered up into the rafters and sat there. Mans and Hild threw their arms about one another. For a while they could hear nothing but the tumult of their hearts.

Some time later they heard Peter speaking to Eyvind his neighbour at the end of the meadow.

Then Hild said, 'Thank God' and crossed herself, and kissed Mans on the throat.

The figures that Hild had glimpsed on the skyline were not horsemen. The tinkers, Jock and Mary, having sold a few cans and trinkets in the north islands, Westray and Eday and Rousay, were returning to their tent in a Hamnavoe quarry.

They went slowly, because Mary could see out of only one eye now and the hillside was pocked with dangerous rabbit-holes.

Jock and Mary had never done worse trade than that summer. The peasants were, if anything, poorer than themselves, for the mercenaries were quartered everywhere in the islands and they paid nothing for what they ate and drank. Also the peasants had never possessed the gift of nourishing themselves with roots and limpets. A can of cold water would keep Jock and Mary tramping for half a day.

The tinkers came over the shoulder of Revay from the north. They stood for a while on the skyline. Jock saw three figures below, two peasants and a scarecrow. (Mary saw a few shifting shadows.) Jock rattled his bunch of cans and yelled, 'Bargains, mistress.' The two peasants began to move slowly, like fated creatures, from the cornfield to the cluster of cottages further down the hill. They went into one cottage and closed the door behind them with a clash.

Jock and Mary came down into the fertile valley. There was not a peasant in sight. All the houses were shuttered. 'Another ruined place,' said Jock. 'They don't even want to hear our stories now.'

'Who's that standing over there?' said Mary, pointing at the scarecrow. 'It's one of them soldiers.'

'It's a scarecrow,' said Jock.

Mary wandered uncertainly across the cornfield towards the scarecrow. She felt the rags and the stick. 'You must be a sergeant, you're that stiff,' she said to the scarecrow. 'Did you lose your horse then, sergeant? You won't be able to do much without your horse, will you, in the way of murder and robbery.'

'Come on,' cried Jock from the road below. 'We must be in Hamnavoe before night. Hurry up.'

'Sergeant,' said Mary, 'have you such a thing now, sergeant, as a ha'penny for a half-blind woman!'

'Leave the scarecrow alone,' said Jock.

'Sergeant,' said Mary, 'it's a very serious crime to lose your horse. Also not to answer when you're spoken to. Where is your axe and your dagger? You will be hanged at sunrise. Meantime I reduce you in the ranks.'

Mary removed the sacking from the scarecrow; it would maybe come in handy for wrapping cans in. Jock could tie it round the jaws of some watchdog. It would maybe mend the roof of their tent some winter night.

'Wait for me,' she shouted to Jock, who was whistling along the road a mile further on. 'Wait. Do you want me to break my arse-bone in the ditch?' She stumbled on into the blind bright day.

The peasants of Revay did not unbar their doors till sunset. When they did they saw that the mill in Marwick, that ground meal for the earl and bishop, was on fire. A few horsemen stood in the tower. Other horsemen ringed the walls. They shouted. They brandished axes. Flames multiplied round the base of the mill. The millpond hissed and steamed. With a noise like thunder one of the great millstones fell through the upper floor. Now there was neither mill nor miller to grind meal for the peasants.

Yet once more, in that terrible summer, Hild crossed herself.

Three nights later a man came to the burnt-out mill. He left his horse to crop the sooty grass beside the burn. He went inside. The man was there all that night. About midnight the peasants of Revay heard a single cry of grief in the darkness.

At first light, when Mans and Prem peeped in, the mill was empty again.

They found, however, a broken sword among the burnt and broken stones.

Prelude to the Invocation of the Dove

The oak door of the bishop's church closed behind three travellers, opened again a minute later, received two more travellers, closed. The five men stood in the cold dark porch. They could no longer hear the sea noises, the whirl and cry of plover, the suck of the ebb, the distant voices of fishermen on the Birsay shore. They stood at the bottom of a deep well of gloom. Their hands touched one another, touched a wall, touched the stone font.

A voice said, 'Wait here, please. I do not know if the bishop will see you. He is busy. I don't know if he even wants to see you. What names will I say?'

They repeated, one after the other, their names: Sighvat Sokk. Finn Thorkelson. Havard Gunison. Hold Ragnarson. Sigurd Kalison.

They knew the hidden voice, though it was very faded now: it belonged to their former teacher, the tawse-swinger, the severe dove, Brother Colomb. Time had not infused new sweetnesses into that voice.

The plainchant began, far away, in the heart of the stone web. *Et de vestemento quid soliciti estis . . .*

'There they go again,' whispered Sighvat Sokk. 'That's one sound I can't abide, especially when I'm feeling cold and hungry, like this morning.' His voice shivered; it sounded small and shrunken in the crepuscular hollow.

The five faces began to glimmer out of the darkness. This was another cause for unease; in the complex web of their relationship many strands had been severed, sometimes savagely; some of them did not care to look some others in the eye, far less speak to them. Shadows still, they drifted apart, they formed two clots in the gloom, one at either end of the nave.

They had ridden separately to Birsay that morning, three by two. In one group were Sigurd Kalison, Sighvat Sokk, Havard Gunison. Hold Ragnarson and Finn Thorkelson had arrived an hour later, just when it had ebbed sufficiently to cross over, a clash and slither of hooves on the loose stones, muted thuds on the sand, silence, the snorts of horses.

On the rocks the Birsay peasant-fishermen were making creels when they arrived. They looked with open curiosity at the gentry. One man knotted his brow at them.

The three and the two had nodded to each other, distantly. Much formal courtesy was required, for they were enemies. They had been enemies for two winters past. Havard Gunison turned in his saddle and spread his arms to show that he had no axe or dagger in his belt. Then all the remaining four jerked the heads of the horses round and spread their arms. It might have seemed that they were long-separated friends wanting to embrace one another. In fact it was only to show that they had kept their promises; no sudden blood would flow that day.

A seal ploutered from a rock into the sea.

Hold Ragnarson nodded towards the steep green island and the wet crazy road that went from shore to shore. The three on the other side nodded. They dismounted; they gave the bridles to the fishermen on the shore; silver coins were given and taken; the horses' heads reared away from the fish-smelling arms. Five horsemen were five footmen (not to say pilgrims, though the church on the other side was the only place they could be going to. The Earl's Hall had been shuttered these past two years). One after the other then they left the firm wet sand for slithers of seaweed and a cluster of rockpools. They spread their arms to balance themselves. They did not speak. Once Sighvat Sokk slid on dulse and tried to steady himself and put his free foot into a pool. He cursed softly with the pain of it . . .

A young monk met them on the other side and led them, three by two, up to the church.

Now here they were, in the dark nave. It was not entirely dark now. They could see a small red glimmer: the sanctuary light.

The groups conversed, three by two, in low voices, yet not so low that the other group could not hear what they were saying. Soon, they realized, it would come to direct speaking; these were the muted beginnings of diplomacy.

' "Doesn't know if the bishop will see us!" ' whispered Sigurd Kalison. 'The bishop knew we were coming. We wrote to him at the end of last week. Others besides us promised to send a message too.'

Silence. *Considerate lilia agri.* Sigurd and Sighvat and Havard waited to hear what their enemies at the other end of the nave had to say.

Finn whispered to Hold, 'No, I had no malt to brew. That never happened before, not even in the year of the short corn. I'll tell you though what I'm hoping to get before I leave here today – Brother Ragn's recipe for the heather wine.'

Their gloom-accustomed eyes saw a dark wedge, the altar: on it a gray glimmer: the bishop's morning chalice.

Silence. *Non laborant.* There was someone else in the church, a whisper and a rustle over by the chancel. Finn and Hold waited for their enemies' contribution to these preliminaries. Hold put out his hand and touched stone. A statue bowed over him.

'My opinion you knew all along,' whispered Sighvat. 'We should never have come here. I did not want it. The less the church has to do with these negotiations the better.'

Silence. *Salomen in omni gloria.*

'Yet the fishing was good off Yesnaby and Hoy last week,' whispered Hold. 'I can tell you this too. My oatfield is looking good. I never saw such green. If only it gets peace to grow.'

Over the shadowy altar now a smear of crimson, like a
sleeping tulip: the covered tabernacle. Finn and Havard crooked
their knees, bowed briefly, from their sides of the nave.

Silence. *Hodie est et cras in clibanum mittitur.*

'But we must,' said Havard. 'The bishop is a landowner too,
like us three, like us five. The bishop is one of us. We must be
unanimous. To leave the bishop out would be to weaken our
hand. It could prove disastrous.'

A blackbird sang outside. It seemed he must be standing on
the window ledge and pouring his heart into the chapel. Finn,
the tallest man, stood on tiptoe. He saw the heaving blob of jet
against the slot of light. The bird deluged the church with burst
after burst, then flew away. The frail ghost-song of the monks
emerged out of that rapture. *Audi filia, et vide et incline aurem.*

The altar defined itself further: tall tarnish, tall wax, six times
repeated, on both sides of the tabernacle. A twist of dark
anguish above: flung arms, transfixed feet, a fallen head: the
crucifix.

It was the turn of Finn and Hold. Finn whispered, 'My son
says to me this morning, "Where are you going?" . . . "To see
the bishop," I said . . . "Where's your axe?" he said. "You'd
better wear your axe," he said. (He's seven years old.) . . . "One
does not go armed into a church," I said. Children have become
very innocent and savage in the past year or two.'

Silence. *Concupiscet rex pulchritudinem tuam.* A fierce voice
whispering, 'I'm here about my eyes.'

Bishop William of Orkney had forgotten that a group of
important farmers and merchant-lairds had written asking to
see him, as a matter of urgency, that morning. He was sitting at
his table writing, in Latin, a homily *Concerning the Two Coats, of
Caesar and of God, that cover Adam's Shame.*

'I will speak first of the coat that is beautiful and comely, yet
subject to the mildew and mothfall of time. It hangs in the Hall,

among other treasures, a garment of great splendour. It has more hues and rainbow dyes than the fated coat of Joseph. Who then shall wear this marvel? A man approved of God and by the people, he shall wear it, and then only on special days, as when, for example, the king his lord is come from ship to shore; or, he sits at the high table for the harvest feast; or, a great victory is to be celebrated. The truth is, it would be inconvenient, not to say foolish, to wear this coat every day, because to take this coat about oneself is to assume a great burden and a yoke. This coat is stiff with jet and golden and scarlet threads, it is a storied garment, one tapestry from throat to ankle: so that a gazer may see the entire fable of the people, from a first hungry outgoing under the aurora borealis to a fertile landfall west in the Orkneys. Yes, and here and there a jewel – an onyx or a ruby – gleams among all this cunning embroidery. So, most of the year, this coat hangs from a silver nail in a locked cupboard in the earl's Hall. "But," the reasonable man will object (he that seeks to discover a purpose in everything, be it rainbow or spider's web), "what is the *use* of such a garment?"

'The answer is, this coat has no practical use whatsoever, being purely symbolical. In a mystical way it gives warmth and dignity not to the chosen wearer alone, it enwraps the whole community. For consider, all the people have contributed to the making of it. The shepherd, he has set aside the sheep of his flock with the whitest finest wool. Certain women have dyed the wool with colours both natural and exotic, and afterwards spun it out on their wheels into long threads. The weaver, he has fixed the same into his loom, and thrown warp upon woof until the desired fable began to take slow shape under flying shuttles. Then arrived tailors who were cunning with shears and with needles. And this merchant, he has given a pearl to be sewn on the coat, and this other, he has given a rough knuckle of silver to be melted down and fashioned into buttons. At last this coat-of-state is worn by the earl on a day of trumpets and high hooves.

'Yes, but there is a deeper sense yet in which it may be said that all the people from the highest to the lowest help in the creation of this marvellous coat. Every lawful transaction in the market-place, every courteous greeting on the road, every civil and charitable act – yes, every time a young man kisses a maid in the harvest field because of the plenitude of the season – whenever these things are done a creative stitch is put upon the mystical garment. Pictures of tranquillity are woven thereon. A crofter with a plough. A fisherman with a net. A monk kneeling. A shepherd with sheep. A merchant despatching a ship. A woman at a hearth-stone. A tinker on the road. Many simple acceptable things sing together in harmony on that garment.

'But conversely, when men of the same community act with malice and pride one towards another, then it may be said that the fabric is endangered. Here and there threads must always be working loose. The fishermen come with cut mouths from the ale-house on a Saturday night. The bread at the croft table never breaks in five equal pieces. Even in the monastery the choirmaster howls at a chorister that sings a note wrong. But these are expected attritions, random incursions of the moth, and there are not wanting instant patches and needles to remedy the matter.

'There it hangs, then, in a cupboard in the great Hall, well guarded, the coat-of-state, symbol of the unity and peace of the people – symbol too of their identity among the tribes of the world, for there is no other coat quite like it. The great farmers are summoned, at the end of summer, to a harvest home. They sit at the board. The poor wait at the gate outside. A trumpet sounds. Their lord enters, that splendour hung about him (their history and their destiny). They raise their cups.

'An ancient curse has lately fallen on Orkney. Two men lay claim to the earldom. The mystical coat-of-state is riven, it comes apart in their hands. The fissure runs through field and croft and family. The son murders his father. Corn is sowed but never reaped. Proud strange horsemen ride through the hills. Beasts are become of more value nowadays than men and women. Nor is this war a mere negation of the peace I have spoken about. There is a black joy abroad, a dance of the deadly sins, a withershin rout. This is a mystery of evil, a consequence of Adam's fall: men who turn from the patterns originated by God desire always to return to nakedness and savagery.

'Now, as to the second coat, it is woven upon no earthly looms . . .'

There was a knock at the door. Brother Colomb put his skull-like head in.

'Five men have come to see you,' he said. 'They said they had written to make an appointment. I left them in the church.'

Bishop William remembered then that he had received a letter three days previously from Havard Gunison. He broke off his meditation upon the second coat of heavenly weave that covers the shame of Adam. He rose to his feet. 'I'll come now,' he said.

The five petitioners in the church could see as well now as if they stood in a barn. Light poured through the tall slotted window where the blackbird had sung; the window was a blue and silver sluice. The sun had come out. They saw the other person in the church, the fierce whisperer. An old creature was kneeling at the altar, her mouth – a few shadows sewn together – going out and in; harsh whispers, rags of devotion, came from it: *Sinners . . . hour of death . . .*

Sighvat Sokk whispered, 'I do not like it. I know priests. These priests will end by taking charge of the whole affair. We should never have come here today at all.'

A door opened and closed. A shadow moved behind the altar. '*Dominus vobiscum*,' said a voice – 'The Lord be with you.' Gulielmus appeared. The bishop came towards them round by the gospel side of the altar. He touched lightly the shawled bent head at the steps. He advanced. 'Welcome to Birsay, gentlemen. I am sorry for having kept you waiting. I had a sermon to prepare.'

'God be with you, too,' said Finn Thorkelson. There were other mumbles of salutation, bows – three by two – from this side of the nave and that.

Silence. *Tota decora ingreditur filia regis.*

'I cannot give you much time,' said the bishop. 'We are all busy here. The hospital is full. The brothers can't take in any more wounded men. They are seldom off their knees, bandaging, praying, putting broth into mouths. You war-men have given us plenty to do. I got your letter, Havard. You wished to see me. What can I do for you?'

Three by two they converged on him. They all began to speak together. The church was filled with an unseemly babble; the high ceiling echoed with the boom of conflicting voices. Finn was saying, 'My lord, all this trouble in the islands—'. Sighvat was saying, 'Remember, the church is not to interfere—'. Hold was saying, 'You're a landowner like us, and—'. Sigurd was saying, 'We hope very much that you'll—'. Havard was saying, 'Hakon and Magnus, the earls, they're—'. But they all spoke together, and all that could be made out was a confused hollow echo under the dome.

The bishop held up his hand over the nodding vehement heads.

'I think,' he said, 'there should be some kind of order, to start with. I take it you haven't come here to make a retreat. Havard, you will speak for the others.'

'My lord,' said Havard Gunison, 'we represent the farmers and merchants here in Orkney.'

'Is that so?' said the bishop. His eyes went from face to face. He remembered them all as schoolboys. Since he had seen them last they had gone on Viking cruises, buried their parents, married, begotten children, beaten their ploughs into uncivil edges, grown poor and angry. He remembered, one after another, five quicknesses under those slowly hardening masks. 'Sigurd Kalison. Hold Ragnarson. Finn Thorkelson. Sighvat Sokk. Havard Gunison.' One after another he clasped their hands warmly. 'You're all welcome back to Birsay. Sighvat, I see your feet are wet again – you'll be wheezing again tonight. You were here three years and you never learned to walk on the rocks properly.'

They smiled all about him; even Sighvat Sokk smiled (though he wished he was beside a fire of wood and peats at home).

Silence. Blazon of sun on the floor. It shifted slowly.

The bishop said, 'Tell me, then: what have you come to Birsay for?'

At that the five tongues broke out again simultaneously. The high ceiling boomed and echoed and yowled. It was more like a drunken market-place than the house of God. Havard was saying, 'The earls, they're ruining us –.' Hold was saying, 'You're a landowner too, Reverend Father, and –'. Sigurd was saying, 'We've banded together, all we farmers and merchants –'. Finn was saying, 'We've been at each other's throats till now, but –'. Sighvat was saying, 'It's not as a *priest* that we want you in with us, but –'.

The bishop's face was as cold as stone. They fell silent in mid-sentence, ashamed of the hellish outcry that was still echoing in the furthest corners of the chapel.

'The men of Babel,' said the bishop at last, 'would have built stronger and higher with a bit of mutual understanding. We'd better start by laying some kind of a foundation. This war in Orkney, that's what you've come about, isn't it?'

They nodded, humbly, all around him.

The voice flashed out at them, 'You won't have come here to receive my congratulations. A fine slaughter-house you've made of Orkney.'

They said nothing.

'Sigurd, Sighvat, Havard,' said the bishop, 'you're Earl Hakon's men, I know that. Hold and Finn, you ride with Magnus Erlendson. It must mean something when five enemies walk together across the seaweed.'

'Father,' said Havard, 'we have a plan that we're certain will bring peace. We very much want you to join us in putting this plan into operation.'

'I am a priest,' said the bishop, 'not a politician.'

'That's right,' said Sighvat Sokk. 'Well spoken, Reverend Father. I quite agree with you. The church would do well to keep out of this.'

'Unless you come in with us, my lord,' said Havard, 'we will not be able to act with such authority. What we need is a solid front of all the landowners of Orkney. You own more land than any of us. In Egilsay, at the conference, you will have a powerful voice.'

'In Egilsay?' said the bishop. 'You are going to do this great thing – whatever it is – in Egilsay. Well, you couldn't have chosen better ground. Egilsay, that means church island, from the Latin *ecclesia* – I'm sure you won't have forgotten that, Sighvat.'

'In Egilsay,' said Havard. 'There is to be a peace conference in Egilsay, on Easter Monday.'

'On Easter Monday,' said the bishop. 'I like that, too.'

'We have come here to invite you to be present at the peace meeting in Egilsay on Easter Monday,' said Havard. 'It is important that you should be there, Father. We do not invite you, we summon you. You must come.'

'I'm sorry,' said the bishop. 'I have no skill in patching up an old coat.'

Silence. *Texturae aurene sunt amictus ejus.* The blackbird had returned to the window. He cocked his head. He was silent.

'Then we should not have bothered to come here at all,' said Finn Thorkelson.

'Except that I'm very pleased to see you after all these years,' said the bishop. 'Sighvat, you've caught a bad cold for nothing . . . Patch upon patch – it's a wonder the old coat hangs together at all.'

Three faces looked across at two. One and all they disliked the tropes and figures and images that churchmen use.

'Well then,' said Sigurd Kalison, 'we will have to go to Egilsay without the blessing of the church.'

'You will not go without that,' said the bishop. 'I will ask the dove to be with you at your conference.'

The dove: another holy image. Their feet shifted on the flagstones. The old woman had moved round the church a bit, following the sun-shaft. She was humped under the statue of Saint Olaf now. She sighed and she muttered. Her eyes. Would the holy saint in his mercy put a bit of light back in her eyes? If not, bad cess to him.

'I will not be coming to Egilsay with you,' said the bishop. 'I will pray for you on Easter Monday. That's all I can do, I assure you. But I should know what I'm praying for. Tell me, what is going to happen in Egilsay on Easter Monday?'

'The old woman,' said Hold Ragnarson, and put his forefinger to his lips.

'Is this what Orkney has been reduced to in the past three years,' said the bishop. 'Old blind ragbag – she's a fitting symbol. It is right that she should be here.'

'Well then,' said Havard Gunison, 'this is what we're going to do in Egilsay on Easter Monday. We are going to force peace on the two earls Magnus and Hakon.'

'No,' said the bishop, 'you can't *force* peace on a situation. All you can do is hold the door open and invite peace to enter.'

'You are too subtle for me, Reverend Father,' said Havard. 'I know nothing about doves and patches. I am a plain man. What we propose is perfectly straightforward. On Easter Monday we've arranged that Earl Hakon and Earl Magnus will meet in the island of Egilsay. It is to be, as I said, a peace conference. The earls are to sail towards the island, one from the west and one from the north, with eight ships each.'

'Not eight ships,' said Hold. 'Two ships.'

'Eight,' said Sigurd.

'Two, I was told,' said Finn.

'No, eight,' said Sighvat.

'That doesn't matter,' said Havard. 'The number of ships hasn't been thrashed out yet. There'll be time enough for that.'

'Two or eight,' said the bishop, 'what is the significance of ships? They'd be better – Hakon and Magnus – going to a peace meeting in one lobster boat.'

'Father, they're *earls*,' said Havard. 'It will be an important event. There will have to be a certain amount of ceremony.'

'Go on,' said the bishop.

'Hakon and Magnus will meet face to face,' said Havard, 'a thing that hasn't happened in fifteen months. All the best lawmen in Orkney will be there. The differences between the earls will be freely and frankly discussed. The cards will be on the table. A peace treaty will be made, with us – the magnates of Orkney – as guarantors. With frankness on both sides, I don't see how anything but good can come out of this.'

'The important thing is this,' said Sigurd. 'We, not the earls, will be in charge of the situation. Nor has the King of Norway been invited to attend.'

The old woman had moved round the church a bit further. She crouched at the stone feet of the Virgin. Would the kind holy Lady see to it that Jock got a rabbit for the fire at night. She was hungry. She must see how bad the eyes were now. Hail Mary.

'Here in Birsay,' said the bishop, 'we will pray for the dove to fall.'

'What dove, father?' said Sighvat.

'A small splash of white among the deluges and the thunder,' said the bishop. 'A branch across the beak, brought we think from the tree of innocence and atonement. A simple blessing on the things that men propose.'

They moved, all six, towards the main door.

'All I know is,' said Finn, 'that there is to be a peace meeting.'

They went out into a blaze of light.

'Peace-making,' said the bishop, 'is at best the patching of an old coat. To make true peace, the *pax Christi*, is to weave the seamless garment.'

One by one, under the arch, they knelt and kissed Bishop William's hand.

Havard Gunison put his knee to the cold stone last. His mouth touched the amethyst. He rose. 'You will not come to Egilsay, Father?' he said.

'No,' said the bishop.

They turned then, the peace-makers. They passed from the church to the salt bitten grass, and on down to the sand and the rocks. The waters encroached slowly. The young seal looked at them with large wise eyes. The old poor-sighted woman was taking whelks from the pools; she groped for the shells; her fingers went like roots among the pebbles. The five men looked across to their horses pacing nervously on the far shore.

The bishop blessed their going.

'So we are to have peace?' said Brother Colomb behind him.

'I do not think their treaty will do much good at all,' said the bishop in a tired voice. 'Perhaps for a month it will, perhaps for ten years. Then it's back with them to the old mischief again. What is needed in Orkney is something more in the nature of a sacrifice, the true immaculate death of the dove.'

The five peace-makers stood on the links on the other side. They received their bridles from the hands of the fishermen. They mounted. They waved curt farewells. They rode away, three by two, in opposite directions.

The Killing

When that the holy season of pasch was overpast, the jarls busked them both for the tryst. The jarl Magnus Erlend's son gathered into two ships leal and trusty and large-hearted men, as many as had been sworn, and held course for Egil's Isle. They sailed upon a calm and a blissful sea-road, but that one billow rose and broke about the helm-bound jarl. Was meikle marvel in the two dove-ships anent that token. And the jarl saith, 'The sign sheweth I fare fast to my life's close. For there will be brought to birth soon a dark foretelling anent the jarl Hakon. Rest ye sure of that. My kinsman Hakon cometh his own gait to this tryst.' Fell then a sudden death-dread upon the ships, and voices that urged return, and hands were held out yearningly towards the hither healthful shore. The jarl Magnus maketh true response, 'Fare yet forward, not I but God is helmsman here.'

I must tell now concerning the jarl Hakon Paul's son, how he summoned about him an host, and set them in eight war-hungry ships. Then those tryst-men heard a great boast, how that from the meeting in Egil's Isle but one jarl would fare him home at sunset, and that not Magnus. A death-lust on listening faces about the mast, a weaving of warped words. Sigurd and Sighvat were the blackest mouths in all that hell-parle. Fierce sea stallions trampled the waves. Who is he that keepeth troth to jarl and jarl, being heart-thirled to both, in the false onset? Havard Guni's son trusts his bitterness to billows, he breasts the surge, to a bare isle he swims where he is sole dweller that night, a cold comfortless man.

*   *   *

Oars rose and fell in the firth. The blades shattered the glass
with regular plangencies. Circular dark wounds marked the
path of the ship *Flame* through the firth, but the sea soon healed
itself again. The oarsmen of *Flame* and *Rockspring* swayed in
rhythm from their haunches; they lay far back, dragging the
blades through the sea; they thrust forward, and then the blades
quivered, scattering light and water-drops. The bows reared
against the horizon with every oar-thrust, and fell back, nuz-
zling the sea; and rose, and fell; and rose, and fell. Oarsmen, the
'spindrift oxen', gave little grunts every time they struck the
water. *Rockspring* surged after *Flame* through the firth.

Finn Thorkelson gently eased the tiller rope, edging the ship a
point to the west. The hull leaned over. Then the oarsmen on
the port side suddenly found their oars buried up to the
rowlocks; their shoulders creaked with the huge weight of
water. The starboard oars skimmed the surface like rapid birds
and sliced off slivers of sea. The oarsmen glowered at Finn
Thorkelson. They swung and dug and grunted, seeking the new
rhythm. The prow of *Flame* was pointing now among the low
islands. The oars rose and fell, rose and fell.

The sea chid gently the straining hull of *Flame*. The ship was
near the centre of a ring of flat or hilly islands: Hrossey,
Eynhallow, Rousay, Gairsay, Shapinsay, Wyre, Eday, Sanday,
Stronsay. Beyond Wyre could be seen a part of Egilsay, mostly
heather and rock; and it was off the lee shore of Egilsay that the
two ships would anchor before sunset, alongside the two ships
of Earl Hakon Paulson. The firth today, gently contained inside
that ring of islands, was a sheen of silver and gray that kept
changing under the changing light of the sky. Outside, beyond
the islands, it was another matter; the voyagers could hear
through the silence a cry and thunder of surf from the west,
where the Atlantic ceaselessly nudged the crags. *Flame* and
Rockspring could not have ridden the sea so easily beyond
Scabra Head or Marwick Head. Even the gentleness of this

inner sea was illusory; it was continually threaded with tides wavering moonwards between the Atlantic and the North Sea, and shrinking again, every twelve hours. If the oarsmen had shipped their blades for a minute *Flame* and *Rockspring* would not have hung tranced on the sea; the Atlantic, thrusting sevenfold between the islands, would have dandled the ships here and there, and underwater springs would have borne them up and given them no rest. They would have been set against this reef, laid upon that shore. The earl had only to glance westward to see a white level cataract of water flooding in on each side of Eynhallow, slumbrous deluges that were mingled now and then with frail carillons and liturgical fragments from the monastery there.

Slowly the islands shifted their places. Earl Magnus could see more of Egilsay now – a few crofts, the kirk on the ridge.

'I have a cramp in my shoulder,' he heard Sem the oarsman shriek suddenly from the starboard bow.

'Flok, put down that pan, take his place,' said Finn Thorkelson quietly.

Flame lost way and fluttered on the water while the groaning man and the boy who had been bailing changed places on the thwart.

Rockspring passed *Flame*. Hold Ragnarson the helmsman of *Rockspring* raised his fist to the sky. The men in *Rockspring* cheered and jeered. Finn Thorkelson gestured *Rockspring* back: the earl's ship must not be passed. *Rockspring* hung on the water with uplifted dripping oars. Light shifted and moved over the firth. The sea around *Flame* was shattered; the ship surged on.

There had been little sleep for Earl Magnus the previous night and now, with the regular strike of the oars and the gentle onset of the ship through the firth, he began to be drowsy. He did not sleep – he was aware of the chink of the bailing pan and the black silk patch on Finn Thorkelson's sleeve – but a 'dream' kept intruding into his consciousness. He had experienced this dream a few times in the past winter; it was not a pleasant dream, it was touched always with shame and loss and sorrow, but always when he opened his eyes afterwards he found that his mind was trembling with expectation. Earl Magnus dropped his head on his chest and yielded to the images that besieged his consciousness (but not for a moment did he cease to hear the swiltering of water and the grunts of the oarsmen as they dug the sea and flung the sklintering flashing blades behind them). The dream intermeshed with his diurnal existence: and it came, as he knew it would, in the form of an invitation – he was summoned in no uncertain terms to attend a marriage, first the ceremony and then the feast. A voice called out in the street below his window. In the dream Magnus had no name. The voice said, 'Thou art required, man, to appear at the nuptial table of the great lord.' The nameless one in the dream was most eager to go, yes and to take with him a suitable gift, something or other that he had made himself and that would be a pleasant thing in the hands of the bridegroom, something that would make the faces of the bride and all the bridesmaids dimple with pleasure. ('Kol, raise your oar a bit higher,' he heard Finn Thorkelson shouting.) But why should the likes of him be invited to a feast, seeing that in the dream he was such a drab ordinary person? It was a bare room he lived in. A brief candle in a wall recess glimmed on poverty everywhere. He had just finished his supper, it seemed; beside the candle there was a crust and a fishbone. He looked with a surge of shame at the clothes he wore – his coat was all stained and torn, there was a splash of dry blood on the breast of it, there were sea-slime and grease and urine marks here and there on sleeves and hem. He dared not go to the nuptial hall of the lord with such a poor thing on his body (and yet it was plain, on closer examination, that originally the coat had been a good one – some knowledgeable tailor must have made it out of the finest gray linen – how had the coat then come to be in its present filthy state, as though it had been trailed through brothels, pig-sties, ale-houses, holds, markets, knackeries?). The shoes of the dreamer were two tattered bits of sealskin. He could not find in that poor hovel water to splash his face, far less a phial of lavender to touch to his beard and arm-pits. Yet the summons had been loud and imperious; he dared not ignore it. He closed the door of his shack behind him. It was night. Here and there about the streets, far off, he heard scattered trumpets summoning other guests. He was very hungry – he looked forward to the fruit and cakes and wine at the bridal board. He moved through a labyrinth of dark streets, going here and there, looking for the festal hall. But there was only darkness, shuttered windows, smells of decay, as if the city had suffered some epidemic or orgy of looting, and he was a survivor of some huge catastrophe. He saw a group of men at the end of a close with lanterns in their hands. He moved towards the illuminated faces but the watchmen looked through him with cold unseeing eyes. For them this wretched creature did not exist . . . It was then, as he turned away, that a sudden flush of joy went through the dreamer. He remembered that in some small weaver's shop in the city he had ordered a length of valuable stuff, a while back. The coat must be ready now, or almost ready. But where in all the huge town was the low raftered cloth-smelling place to be found? He could not remember ever having seen the face of the weaver; he had the impression that he was a young man; and always, when he tried to imagine that anonymous hidden one with his frame and coloured wools, there came an infusion of sweetness into his mind, as if he was recalling some dear, removed, half-forgotten friend of his childhood. Well then, the coat ordered so long ago must surely be ready now. He would take the new coat about his body like a swathe of light. But where was the weaver's shop? He remembered, trembling, that to get to it he had to pass through a terrible street – a shambles with the reek of guts and blood, a place of fires and burning. Beyond those dangerous doors was the tranquil loom . . .

There was a sudden frightful commotion on board *Flame*. The oarsmen fell against one another. Earl Magnus was shaken awake by a slash of spindrift across his face. Bailing pan and anchor clanged together amidship. Finn Thorkelson was thrown down on his knees and elbows. The rudder swung free. A segment of sea sifted over, fell into the ship with a crash. *Flame* was upborne by a single huge wave, then set down once more, shuddering, on the glassiness. The undulation, one solitary wayward lump of sea, passed under and away. The oarsmen sat up, disentangled the oars, looked at one another with bewildered faces, looked at the freak wave that was even now flattening out, squashing itself unevenly over the neutral surface. It was as if some underwater fountain had burst open and as suddenly subsided.

Once again *Rockspring* passed them. The wave had not come near her. The men on *Rockspring* cheered and shook their fists.

The earl's tongue touched the crust of salt at the corner of his mouth. The islands had shifted around him slightly since he had fallen half-asleep in the stern. Now fire burned here and there on the hills of Rousay; gray smoke-strands, slowly unravelling, drifted across the heather; the peasants were exercising, as every spring, their rights of muirburn.

Finn Thorkelson, the tiller-rope once more in his hand, stood wet and silent and perturbed.

'So,' said Earl Magnus, 'it was an omen. The wave was a signal from Fate. We are not to proceed. Something frightful and unfortunate will happen if we land on Egilsay today. At the very least the negotiations with Earl Hakon will not be a success. The wave was a warning to us.' His face shone from the washing of the sea. He smiled.

'I am inclined to think so,' said Finn Thorkelson. 'I will signal to Hold Ragnarson in *Rockspring*.'

The boy Flok blundered about the ship with his bailing can. He emptied canful after canful of the ominous wave back into

the wholesome waters. 'I think you are quite right,' said Finn
Thorkelson. 'We will turn back at once.'

Some of the oarsmen thought so also. They looked over their
shoulders towards Egilsay. They looked between the hill fires of
Rousay and the black plough-patches on Wyre. They looked at
Magnus and Finn, waiting for the order to turn the ship round.
The rhythm of the oar-strokes slackened.

'Row, you sons of whores,' cried Finn Thorkelson. '*Rockspring* is in front. Row until you're ordered to stop. Row,
bastards, till you drop.'

He bent over Magnus and said in a low voice, 'My lord, I
think in all seriousness we should turn back. It is foolishness, to
ignore such an extraordinary phenomenon, a single sudden
mountain of salt in a salt plain. It almost swamped us. I know
that nowadays we are more enlightened than our old pagan
grandfathers who saw Fate in the falling of a leaf. But this that
has happened just now is altogether unique – I have never in
forty years of sailing about in this firth experienced anything
like it. The sea has uttered a warning. It may be that nature has a
wisdom and a knowledge hidden from men.'

'Finn,' said Earl Magnus, 'tell me this, why am I going to
Egilsay today?' His tongue burned with the salt. Another drop of
sea water oozed from his hair, ran down his forehead into his
eye. His vision blurred, reformed. He looked at the land and the
sea with washed eyes.

'There is to be the signing of a formal peace treaty between
Earl Hakon Paulson and yourself,' said Finn Thorkelson. 'It has
all been arranged down to the last detail. Today you are going to
put the seal on it.'

'That too,' said Earl Magnus. 'But there's this wedding feast.
There's this coat that I ordered a while ago. I hope I'll have time
to see to these things when I'm in Egilsay.'

'I see,' said Finn.

'And you don't turn back from the weaver's door,' said

Magnus, 'nor from the loaded table, just because your feet are wet.'

God help us, thought Finn Thorkelson. God help the people of Orkney who have an incompetent like this in charge of their affairs. God help the fishermen and the ploughmen . . . And Finn thought it was unfortunate that his farm wasn't in that part of Orkney that was ruled over, with firmness and common sense, by this one's cousin. A wedding – a coat for a wedding – for God's sweet sake!

There was a shout from *Rockspring*. It came shivering and sweet over the intervening sea. They looked. Hold Ragnarson was standing up in the stern. He was pointing with a rigid arm towards Egilsay. The islands had shifted round them, mute protective presences. They could see almost the whole island of Egilsay now. There were no other ships in the bay. *Flame* and *Rockspring* had arrived before the two ships of Earl Hakon Paulson.

'Keep pulling,' said Finn to the oarsmen. 'We're almost there.'

Rumours of new dramatic developments in the peace confrontation between the Paulson faction and the Erlendson faction have been coming from this lonely isle all through Sunday night and this morning. The parties themselves are maintaining strict secrecy, but that something unexpected has happened is beyond doubt. There is a black-out of news. Neither of the parties is willing to give anything away. Through interviews with crofters and fishermen and their wives we have been able to build up a fairly definite picture, though an outline here and there, in the absence of any statement from either the Paulson or the Erlendson camp, remains vague.

The Paulson–Erlendson deadlock seemed, a week ago, to be as intractable as ever, with all its bloody and tragic repercussions. Tentative peace overtures have been made from time to time, of course, in the past sixteen months. But last week it seemed that a firm basis for negotiation had been arrived at, when high-ranking envoys of both parties came together in the cathedral church of Birsay in the north-west of Orkney, in a meeting convened by the Bishop. Leading the Paulson delegation were Sigurd Kalison, Sighvat Sokk, and Havard Gunison. Finn Thorkelson and Hold Ragnarson negotiated on behalf of the Erlendson faction. All that remained to do was to bring the real leaders together, to tidy up a few loose ends, and to put the actual signatures on the treaty. The venue for this final scene was widely known – the rather barren and featureless island of Egilsay, which lies in a fairly neutral position between the Paulson and Erlendson power spheres.

The fact that both leaders were to be present in Egilsay marked a highly significant development: Paulson and Erlendson have never seen or communicated with each other personally for upwards of three years.

It is now certain that both leaders are, in fact, in Egilsay. Our correspondent has spoken to many of the islanders. Arkold Sweynson of the croft of Flinders saw the first peace vessels arrive. 'I was down at the beach getting a bit of driftwood for my fire when I saw two launches approaching between Rousay and Wyre. This would have been in the middle part of the day. They dropped anchor in Skaill bay. There must have been upwards of a score of men in them. They weren't pleasure boats and they weren't fishing boats either. They must have cost a fine lot of money. Whatever they were, I thought it was time for me to get off home. I watched the crews coming ashore in small boats from the end of my house. Most of the island folk had come out and they were standing watching, like myself, at their doors. Well, we didn't know who they were, right enough, but there didn't seem to be any guns at all, and we were all just wondering, I suppose, what they were wanting in Egilsay.' . . .

Valt Gunnarson of Asteath told our reporter that some of the strangers had lit a fire at the shore first of all. They all seemed to be quite friendly disposed. 'One or two of them waved their arms to the island folk, but I didn't see anybody waving back. Well, we still didn't know what they were. You have to be careful nowadays. The next I saw, one of the men walked through the fields up to the summit of Egilsay. We haven't got anything you could call a hill. He stood there for more than an hour, looking with binoculars north and east. Then a few of the strangers walked up the beach and over the fields in the direction of the crofts. I thought it best, just to be on the safe side, to go in and bar the door. You never know, there's been all this trouble and fighting in some of the islands. I thought I recognized one of the men from seeing his photo in the papers, Magnus Erlendson, but I couldn't be sure.' . . .

Torf Shuttle, a weaver, of Stedquoy, was one of the few islanders who didn't know that anything unusual was happening in Egilsay yesterday. 'I went to the kirk in the morning, seeing it was Easter Sunday. That's generally the only time of the year I go to the kirk now, that and Christmas. Well, I was having this bite to eat before the fire, after the service, when this knock comes to the door. I turned and I saw three men standing there. I didn't know them from Adam. I invited them in. You never know, they might have been wanting to buy a bit of tweed. One of the men asked me what kind of a living I made. I said, very bad, with the times troubled like they were. This same man seemed to be interested in my loom and the bit of stuff I was weaving. The others never said a thing. This man asked me some questions about it. He knew a bit of what he was talking about all right. They left after a short while. They didn't buy a thing. The man who did the talking said he hoped there would soon be better times for the Orkney folk. I didn't know till later that he was Magnus Erlendson.' . . .

Sara Meldotter is a widow who lives in Glebefield, another croft. She also had a visit from the strangers. 'I was baking oatcakes on the range,' she said. 'I just happened to look up and there was this three men standing in the door. I didn't know who they were. One of the men came into the kitchen. The other two bade outside. I was black affronted, I can tell you, everything in a stir-up and the kitchen full of the reek of baking. I must say he was a very nice civil man. The other two just hung about the door. I didn't know at the time that the man was Magnus Erlendson. I was only told that later. Well, I offered him an oatcake and a bowl of ale. He said a funny thing, "I'm ashamed to take this because I've trampled your corn into the earth." I've never grown oats or barley this long while, not since my man died. I get a stone of meal whenever I need it from the miller. However he took the oat bannock and broke it, and he said, "Let there be peace from now on between the folk of Orkney and me." He made some kind of a sign over the oatcake, then he ate all the pieces, one after the other, down to the last crumb, and he drank the ale. I found a bit of silver on the dresser after he left. I hadn't asked him for anything.' . . .

Our reporter spoke to two 'travelling people' who happened to be in the island. Mrs Mary O'Connell has been almost totally blind now for five years but she enjoys an occasional smoke from her clay pipe and a dram. She said she had never lived in a stone house in her life. 'Jock and I came here to Egilsay because we heard rumours a week ago that there was likely to be a crowd of "toffs" in Egilsay this weekend, and "where there's folk there's pickings." ' . . .

Mord Clack of the Mill said it was a complete surprise to him, these strangers coming to the island on a Sunday in spring. They got a few tourists in the summer, but never generally so early as this. The first he knew of it was when he saw the fire at the shore. Then he saw the three men going between Torf Shuttle's place and Glebefield. 'I thought it best in the circumstances to go inside and bar the door. I have a wife and five children. I saw this other man on the top of the hill through my window. He was looking north through binoculars like one of them birdwatchers. He had been there for a good hour and more. He was standing quite still. All of a sudden I saw him waving his arms. He seemed to be very excited about something. He kept shouting and pointing north. He ran half way down the fields. Two of the other three men went running up across the fields to meet him. It was a calm day and I could hear plainly what he was shouting. "Eight boats! I've seen them! Eight full boats!" All three of them seemed to be very excited when they met at the burn above my house. They all went back up to the summit of the island and they looked northwards for some time. I couldn't help noticing this other man, the one who had been going round from croft to croft. He didn't seem to be put out at all by what was exciting the other men. There he was, all by himself down at the shore. He was whistling to one or two seals on the rocks below. Then I saw some of the other men that had come in the boats in the morning running up from their fires to the top of the island. They seemed to be very much excited too. I didn't know what was happening. I thought it best to close the shutters.' . . .

Mund Voes, fisherman, said that he had no idea what was going on. 'It's got nothing to do with me,' he said. 'I have my living to make out of the sea. I can't drop everything and gape, like some folk, just because a few strangers come to Egilsay. My fishing yawl was on the shore that afternoon. I had been painting her most of the week before to be ready for the lobsters. I went down with a tin of paint to touch up her name on the bow – *Jemima*. I was hoping to set a few creels the next day off the west of Rousay. I had seen the two yacht-type boats come in at the pier earlier on. It had nothing to do with me. I met a sailor off one of the yachts and we smoked a cigarette together beside my boat. He told me he was one of the Erlendson lot. I hadn't asked him. It was none of my business who he was. He said there was going to be some kind of a show-down next day with the Paulsons. He asked me not to tell anybody, it was still a kind of a secret. I told him I didn't care anyway, so long as nobody interfered with me or my business. Somebody from further along the shore shouted this chap's name. He gave me a drink out of his half-bottle he had in his hip pocket, then he went back to join his mates. He was quite a decent bloke. I finished painting the name of the boat. The weather looked fairly settled. I went home as it would be an early start for me in the morning. There was a lot of shouting going on here and there in the west end of the island, a coming and a going between the shore and the hill. All the crofts were barred and shuttered, I suppose to be on the safe side. I saw a small crowd of strangers round the manse door. The manse seemed to be the centre of all the activity on the island at that particular time, about five in the afternoon. Some kind of a palaver was going on between a few of the strangers and the missionary. I wasn't going to lock my door for anybody. I didn't intend to lose any sleep either. I live alone. I got up to relieve myself about two-thirty in the morning and then I saw this light in the church. Jon Skate and I got the *Jemima* into the water at five o'clock in the morning. When we were pushing off I saw there were these eight other strange boats anchored further out in the bay. Jon Skate is the man I fish with. The island was swarming with men in the first light. They were everywhere. They seemed to be in two main groups, one down on the shore and the other on the slope above the kirk. Well, Jon Skate and I set our creels and we had a pint in Rousay before we made for home. Everybody in Rousay wanted to know what was happening over in Egilsay. There was a lot of excitement. Personally, I don't give a damn about their politics and their carry-on. Jon Skate and I had got a few lobsters. When I went up to 'phone to the Fishermen's Society in Hamnavoe I couldn't get through. Brenda Freyson is the postmistress. She told me the line had been cut.' . . .

The island missionary, Mr Andrew MacPhail, refused to say anything to our reporters. He did agree that a man had spent all the previous (Sunday) evening in his manse, and afterwards in the church. He refused to identify the man as Magnus

Erlendson. He refused to say if the man was still in the church or not.

The situation is still confused. But a picture is beginning to emerge. What is certain is that if an agreement is signed sometime today it will hardly be in the spirit of last week's Birsay preliminary talks. It will be a settlement dictated by Hakon Paulson, who arrived in Egilsay late yesterday afternoon (Sunday) with an impressive backing of boats and men with guns.

The time then that this priest was at the altar, below the crucifix, between two lighted candles, standing, stooping, genuflecting, striking his breast thrice in sorrow – so it was said – for his own sins and for the sins of all the world, while this action was going forward in the kirk, outside the rim of the sun touched the hills of Rousay in the west, and the kirkyard stones were caught in a net of shadows, and the little crofts begot black bulwarks of darkness; then it was that a mouthless shadow from the darkling world entered into the kirk and passed through clusters and enfoldings of shadow about the west door where the font was; and inside because of the oncoming night still taller rose the candle flames and threw quiet lavings of light on old stonework, and now that the time had come for the old priest to say the Gloria, the twilight within had a wavering garment of richness flung upon it.

At the north wall of the kirk knelt the man who had entered. He put a bleak look on the altar from time to time, then tilted his head into his hands as if he were praying. But his mouth was not praying, it was trying to accommodate itself to a sudden taste of ashes. Palms and forehead generated a sweat about his face (though it was cold in the kirk). His knees were of stone where they touched the stone floor. And when he turned his face once towards the altar to see what the priest was doing (the priest was asking for his heart to be made pure so that his lips could worthily utter the gospel: so it was said and so the man had once believed) then the two candles on the altar hollowed out the man's cheeks and temples, and made pits of his eyes, and dissolved in light the russet fringe that circled his face, so that it seemed the man had left his life and was already gone half way along the road of the skull.

Then the old priest peered closely into the parchment that he held in front of him, and he read the Latin in a faded voice. Eye and tongue went together, hesitant, over the characters in the script, the single initial character that had once been gorgeously dyed and stained like a butterfly's wing and the ruck of black characters. Candle-light splashed the worn parchment. The voice sighed and was silent, and went on again. The piece of the gospel that the old priest read was that parable in which Christ compares the celestial kingdom to a marriage feast, and how it is good for a guest to wear to the feast his wedding garment lest, having some inferior garment on, he is shamed and put out into the darkness where drift, in ignorance and sorrow, those benighted who have no proper habitation in time or in eternity.

The priest finished the reading and put on the parchment his parchment mouth. A brief interest had kindled in the man's stiff face while the gospel was being read, a gleam of recognition; that faded; now he went down once more upon his knees and tried to mingle the pain he felt with the action which was going forward at the altar, namely the receiving by the priest of the bread and wine that the people now offered to God, the work of their hands; for an orison at such a time – so he had once believed – has special sweetness and power; but all that his lips found to whisper was an old moth-eaten formula. *Now my good angel whom God has appointed to be my guardian watch over me during this night;* and it was all a crunching of cinders in his mouth. He was possessed by such a sense of abandonment and such a lassitude that no kindly breath, he thought, could ever kindle his mouth again to a fervent flame of praise.

Yet the man found a little comfort in meditating on the mystery of what was happening there at the altar (as some old story might comfort a child on a winter night). It was a slow cold formal dance with occasional Latin words – an exchange of gifts between God and man, a mutual courtesy of bread and wine. Man offers – so this worshipper had believed hitherto, at all events – the first-fruits of his labour to the creator of everything in the universe, stars and cornstalks and grains of dust. This is not to say however that man is simply a brutish breaker of furrows, but he labours well in a variety of trades also, with stone and with loom and with oar and with harp and with law-book and with sweet orderings of words and with prism, towards some end which is likewise a kind of harvest. Well he knows that he could not call himself man at all unless he labours all his time under the sun to encompass the end for which his faculties were given him. This end, whatever the nature of his occupation, is his harvest time; and he would be a poor labourer that would not wish, among all that broken gold, to offer back a tithe or a hundredth into the hands that formed the original fecund dust. Yet many a labourer there is whose hands and mouth are stilled before he can gather in the fruit of his labours, and what happens to such a one who is called away untimely into the darkness, at the season of the braird it may be, or when the full ear of corn has not yet broken from the shoot? With bitterness he will turn from the sun and the faces of his children. Yet even so the corn does not fail, there are hands that will bring a portion of the bread that the dead man has sown from barn to kirk in the time of thanksgiving; and the bread will be broken, and suffused with divine essences, and the mouths that taste it shall shine for a moment with the knowledge of God. For the generations, and even the hills and seas, come and go, and only the Word stands, which was there – all wisdom, beauty, truth, love – before the fires of creation, and will still be there inviolate among the ashes of the world's end.

Untimely death might still, in retrospect, seem good and acceptable (in spite of all). What of the husbandman who is cut down by sudden scythes in the middle of his glebe? The man's heart knocked thrice, a slow heavy assault, on his side. His brow glittered. His mouth was ashes. His mouth was dust and salt.

The man, to distract himself, sought to enter deeper into the significance of what was happening at the altar. The Mass was not an event that takes place in ordinary time, like eating a fine dinner in some hall, or sailing in a boat between two islands, or sharpening an axe; wherein the participant is a little more withered and ripe at the end than at the beginning (such are the desiccations and renewals and subtle minute engravures of time); it takes place both in time, wherein time's conditions obtain, and also wholly outside time; or rather, it is time's purest essence, a concentration of the unimaginably complex events of time into the ritual words and movements of a half-hour. A loaf of bread is a fitting symbol for agricultural man. The blood and sweat that men have given to secure their nourishment and cheer come at last to this simple shape on a table. The bewildering babel of languages in every country since Eden, by which men strive to understand themselves and their human condition and things that cannot be properly understood but only wondered at and celebrated (being too subtle for understanding) are touched to silence in the Mass; they are resolved into a few secret whispers. If – the man thought dully – we could look with the eye of an angel on the whole history of men, *sub specie aeternitatis*, it would have the brevity and beauty of this dance at the altar.

The end and the beginning. All time was gathered up into that ritual half-hour, the entire history of mankind, as well the events that have not yet happened as the things recorded in chronicles and sagas. That is to say, history both repeats itself and does not repeat itself. One event; one group of characters that move in and through and out of the event, and both make

the event and are changed by it, collectively and individually –
that event bears resemblances to another event that occurred a
hundred years before, so that a man listening to a saga is moved
to say, 'This is the same performance all over again.' It is not:
the costumes have changed, the masks have changed, the
gestures though similar have a new style, and the personages
will soon go away into their own mysterious silence. Events are
never the same, but they have enough similarity for one to say
tentatively that there are constants in human nature, and
constants in the human situation, and that men in similar
circumstances will behave roughly in the same fashion.

Poetry, art, music thrive on these constants. They gather into
themselves a huge scattered diversity of experience and reduce
them to patterns; so that, for example, in a poem all voyages –
past, present, and future – become The Voyage, and all battles
The Battle, and all feasts The Feast. This is to look at those
events of time which resemble one another yet are never quite
the same, in a symbolical way. The symbol becomes a jewel
enduring and flaming throughout history. Therefore all our
little journeys and fights and suppers that seem so futile once
they are over, are drenched with the symbol, and retain a
richness they never had while they were being experienced. Men
handle the jewel and know themselves enriched.

But the symbol remains an abstraction. The sacrament deals
with the actual sensuous world – it uses earth, air, water, fire for
its celebrations, and it invests the creatures who move about
among these elements with an incalculable worth and dignity.
Sacramentally seen, the poorest beggar is a prince, every peasant
is a lord, and the croft wife at her turning wheels of stone and
wood is 'a ladye gaye'. From the christening water to the last oil
those immortal creatures move about in a world unimaginably
rich; and the most precious times of the turning year are the
feast days when these peasants with the stigmata of labour on
their bodies enter as noblemen into 'the kingdom of the ear of

corn': that is, when they experience with their actual senses the true dignity of the work they do, kneeling and receiving their own bread, made divine, into their mouths. The body–spirit dichotomy, or the body–intellect dichotomy, is a bitter prideful cleaving of the wholeness of a man's nature. Earth and man and sun and bread are one substance; they are made out of the original breath-smitten dust. Men must never despise the flames and darknesses they have come from. The best earth-gold is the cornstalk in August.

Since all the round of time is gathered into this ritual half-hour, the actions of Everyman, once the bread of divine wisdom is in his body, have an immense importance; what he does and says and thinks reverberates through the whole web of time. Men not yet born will be changed, either for good or ill, by his speech and the things that his hands find to do (as seapink and star tremble to one another's motions). A man can therefore direct his purified will into the future for the alleviation of the pain of the future. The pain of the dead (the man knew) is soothed by a healing word or thought. But perhaps the pain of all history might be touched with healing by a right action in the present. Especially in an evil time, when all the furrows are disordered, a chosen man might have to mingle himself with the dust, until once more the sun and the conflagration of ripeness at the earth's centre burn together in his blood. The man whispered, and the whole web of history trembled. He breathed out pain on the gray air. Two images came unbidden into his mind. He saw himself in the mask of a beast being dragged to a primitive stone. A more desolate image followed, from some far reach of time: he saw a man walking the length of a bare white ringing corridor to a small cube-shaped interior full of hard light; in that hideous clarity the man would die. The recurrence of pattern-within-flux touched him, momentarily, with wonder.

But his spirit was too cold to be warmed any more by that subtle weave of imagery. The Mass today was simply the

movements of an old man and a boy. The boy was taking a cruet
of wine and a cruet of water from the window embrasure. The
boy was giving these trifles to the old man. The old man
mingled liquid with liquid. The old man muttered a few dead
foreign words.

The bitter cold of the church had in the past few minutes
branched like a frozen fountain through all the man's being.
Terror generates a supernatural cold. Cold ground out of cold
first a slow languor, then a dream; or rather the figures and
shapes that moved in the man's mind were the resumption of a
dream he had had, in a ship, earlier that day, concerning a royal
marriage feast and the unworthiness of a certain guest to take
his place at the table; and how he had set out to find the good
weaver who was making a coat for him; but the dream had
petered out in a sickening slaughter-house stench. What the
man dreamed now in the kirk was a part of the same dream,
certainly, but touched with deeper sorrow and denial. He was
one of a great shoal of mouths that drifted in front of a
magnificent courtyard. They were neither men nor spirits, they
were blind mouths crying at the gate of a palace that was forever
shut against them. The mouths were hungry. They longed to eat
the food that was being served at the long tables, the pleasant
bread and the honey and the tender savoury meats; they longed
to drink the wine that was being poured out of a tall jar into
silver goblets. Inside the hall the eating and the drinking were
part of an endless bounty and courtesy; voices greeted each
other gladly from table to table; there was the sound of a lute,
there was the sound of the feet of a dancer. The mouths of the
benighted outcasts were gross, like the snouts of swine. None of
them was worthy, the dreamer concluded, to taste the king's
bread; and furthermore he knew that unless he and all the
others tasted it they would drift about forever outside, in ever-
deepening darkness and cold, savage never-satisfied immortal
hungers. (So, he had not after all been able to find the weaver's

workshop – perhaps he had not had the courage to walk through the street of butchers to the song of the loom – he must have turned back without his new coat to find the wedding hall, obedient to the invitation, and on the way there he had mingled with large and small groups of these other hungers going the same way, all whispering eagerly that at least they would be given the scraps and dregs that were left over.) Nor, the dreamer observed, were they by any means the voices of poor people only – it was a mingling of classes; in their distress they had shed all distinctions, and here and there was a mouth that had gold glitters in it, and a mouth with a fine soft sensuous curve to it, and a mouth that uttered well-turned witty phrases, and even one that commented on their situation in clerical Latin. The mouths eddied back and fore now in the square outside the lighted palace. Sometimes a throb of hope went through those rejected ones, there was a whisper that the doors were about to be thrown open. They seethed with expectation then. In the following silence a mouth put itself to another use: cursing. It cried out against the guests inside; it gave vent to bitter self-reproachings, it remembered happy former springtimes, it cursed the day of its birth, it charged certain others with bringing it to this doorway of flame: mother, wife, children, creditors, friends. That voice was answered with weeping and counter-curses. In darker corners of the square mouths put themselves to still other uses. The dreamer heard lascivious sighs, kissings and slobberings and lewd whispers in doorways, sniggers, pleadings, bitings. Another rumour went through the crowd – they were after all (they acknowledged) the citizens of a defeated allegiance; the royal horsemen had been ordered to sweep them from the square back to their hovels. 'Not I,' said the dreamer, 'I am invited to the feast, I am simply waiting until my new coat is ready for me to wear', but his cry was lost in a low wail from all those withered immortal lips. The dreamer had been troubled ever since he arrived in the square by a nagging gnat-like voice that seemed at first to be speaking to itself only; it uttered nothing but toneless obscenities and blasphemies, over and over again, concerning what was happening inside the hall, a litany of pure filth. The dreamer tried to shake himself clear of it, but the tongue followed him wherever he went, as if its only desire was to convince him that the unsullied splendour inside the hall was not for him, and the sooner the dreamer realized it and reconciled himself to his state of wretchedness the better it would be for him. Indeed the invitation he had got to the marriage feast was nothing but a piece of gratuitous mockery. And if this weaver he kept speaking about was such a good and a trustworthy and a pleasant friend, why had he not – seeing that it was the night of the feast, and the garment so necessary – sought out the dreamer and put the beautiful coat into his hands? The truth was, there was no such weaver and no such coat. Finally this mouth fell to a hellish utterance of profanity and blasphemy. The dreamer tried to answer. His lips moved. They clashed faintly upon each other. His mouth was two bars of ice. He longed to utter some single word that might cancel all that hideous yowling in the square. The cold intensified. There was a word but he could not think what it was. His lips were frozen one on the other. The word the dreamer wanted to utter – whatever it was – would in any case be meaningless here. The shoal of mouths that eddied and swirled everywhere in the darkness suddenly turned all one way, they hung in silence upon the door of the hall. They burned. Something it seemed was about to happen. The king – a new quick whisper went – was about to appear.

The sound of the sacring bell summoned the man out of his dream. The farm boy knelt beside the priest, the bronze wavered in his hand, a small triple resonance was shaken from it. The man was conscious first of his mouth – it was not spirit yet – it was red and it reeked with breath in the kirk. This dust that had drifted so mysteriously into time, his mouth, was still upborne and surrounded by a harmonious congregation of other members – hand, eye, belly, ear, throat, genitals, brain, lungs – all beaten through with a slow wondering pulse – a seventy-year-long pledge (across an earth wound that might be furrow or womb or grave) of history and of time as yet unimaginable and unrealized. The man dug his teeth into his lower lip – he felt a stab of pain. There was still time – his mouth could still utter the unique music of that cosmos of dust that flourished and withered about it; and sign his unique inscape on the listening air. He would not leave this island alive. His mouth was eager now to make, quickly, before it was dust once more, some kind of a response to the hoarded experiences of his fifty-four years. It would have to acknowledge (since it was true) that he had been a bad husbandman – his estate was in utter ruins – the islands he had been given the governance of were ravaged and rutted with war, disease, death – he had come with empty hands to the feast . . . Every grain is purest gold when the dust in the hourglass is whispering, threading, dwindling down to nothingness. The coldness remained, but only corporeally (the blue marbled hands, knees soldered on stone, the shivering mouth). His mind took the small infusion of peace that comes after every hard decision. He offered all that he had left: the peace and the pain.

With difficulty, for that he was an old man and his bones full of stiffness, the priest raised high the Bread of Heaven (for in the Mass, after the angels have borne up to the tables of heaven the mortal bread of man's sowing and reaping and baking – a tithe of his labour – that same bread by the utterance of five words is drenched, interwoven, imbued, possessed, informed with divinity, and is sent down again to be immortal food for the souls of men) and some of it, at any rate, the man now believed.

The chalice was elevated. The priest mingled the broken bread with the wine, figuring forth Christ's resurrection – the man smiled at the beauty of the symbolism. The priest consumed the Host. A moment later he set the Precious Blood to his lips. All things, thought the man, are being done well and in order. The dust that was his mouth opened and shut on the word he could not find in the dream: *Sanctus*. The word pulsed like a star in the murk of the nave.

The farm boy went down on his knees and took the Host into his young mouth from the twisted hand of the priest.

The man heard a stir behind him. There was somebody else in the kirk, kneeling by the door. The man trembled with cold and expectation. The priest looked at him, touched with one finger a Host in the paten: he was being summoned again to a feast of unimaginable splendour and majesty. Dare he go, empty-handed and naked as he was? This much was true, the priest had shriven him before the Mass; he had laid aside the patched filthy coat of sins that he had brought with him to the island.

His mouth had been among hosts of evil; it had been one of them; it had shaken clear. Might it not still be capable of experiencing this good before it died (but in a veiled way, since human flesh would shrivel in that other flame, glory)?

The presence behind him and a little to the right, in the darkest corner, said in a clear voice, 'Go now, man.'

The man rose from his knees. He went up to the altar rail. A coarse oaten crumb – *Corpus Christi* – shone between his lips for a moment. He was a part of the feast.

The man knelt, smiling, his eyes veiled with blue lids. He felt secure then, like a guest in a lamp-splashed jubilant castle.

> Christ around me
> Christ before me
> Christ beside me
> Christ above me

It pleased him to think that when he turned away from the altar he would see, standing at the back of the kirk, the unknown friend. He imagined hands smelling of sandalwood and oil-of-wool.

The man crossed himself. He rose from his knees. He turned. The kirk was empty. His friend was not there. Instead he saw, in the shadows of the porch, the quick flash of a sword and a livid mask above it. Sword and face withdrew at once into the darkness. He listened. A voice called from the next field. The syllables fell among the tombstones. A nearer voice answered.

Ite, missa est, sang the old priest.

The Mass was over. The priest stepped down from the altar and approached the man and said to him, '*Ite, missa est.* That is to say, my lord, "Go now, carry the peace of Christ into the world." . . . But I think it would be best for thee to stay in the kirk tonight, for here in the sanctuary no man can harm a hair of thy head. And indeed, lord, it would be wise of thee to bide here until this madness dies down in the island. They cannot keep their rage for ever. They will have to go home soon to attend to their ships and their farms. There is food and fire for two in my small house. Indeed there is no limit to the time thou canst bide here.'

The man said he thought he would stay until morning. He had a friend in the island and he thought he might see him again in the fields.

The man asked the priest then whether he had seen another man in the church, kneeling somewhat behind him, a man with a very sweet and comely countenance. It could be that the man was carrying a white linen garment.

The priest said with a shaking of his head that there had been nobody in the kirk but three of them – priest, acolyte, worshipper. Sometimes it happened, in a time of trouble, that a man would know the palpable presence of the good guardian angel at his shoulder.

The priest said that neither had he seen a soldier with a sword in the porch. He had been too busy with *In principio erat verbum.*

The man said he thought he would wait in the kirk till the sun got up. Then he would go down to the shore. He had not spoken to a fisherman since he had come to the island.

Finn Thorkelson said they were glad to have found the men they were looking for at last. It was a very dark night and the stones of the shore had been slippery. Leif Mole had fallen and hurt his leg. It had been a good idea of Sigurd Kalison's to suggest that they do their talking not on the beach but in the interior of the island, even though it seemed to be a bleak enough place; for by so doing they formed themselves into a kind of assembly, a 'ting', a parliament, and they were no longer simply an argumentative rabble between the sea and the rocks. There was even a large stone embedded in the earth, beside which a speaker might stand; the stone served as a kind of focal point for the night's proceedings, and gave a certain authority to the words of the speaker. This meeting on the hillside, therefore, would invest their debate, which he trusted would be fruitful, with a semblance of legality. He took it upon himself to speak first, not only because Earl Hakon Paulson's representatives seemed not to be eager to open the debate, but also because he had certain weighty and urgent matters to raise. It was obvious first of all that some mistake had been made. Mistakes however, as they all knew, were an everyday occurrence. You might send a girl down to the pond to bring in a couple of ducks for dinner – an unexpected guest having arrived – and back the silly creature came with *three*. He remembered well asking a dealer to bid for a young bull on his behalf at the Firth market. The man came over the hill in the evening driving a full-uddered cow (as if his wife's cupboard wasn't crammed with butter and cheese already). Things like that were always happening. He could see well enough what had happened in this particular case, how the mistake had come about. It was simply a clerical error. A clerk had sat at his desk in Westray in a dwam about some girl or other who had kissed him the night before. Mister Goosequill had written 'eight' instead of 'two' on the letter he had despatched to Earl Hakon confirming this present meeting. That at least was the explanation that occurred to him, Finn Thorkelson. He saw at any rate that his friends who had come ashore on the opposite side of the island had had a good supper. The air down at the beach had been a tangle of delicious smells. He trusted with all his heart he could still call them friends.

Sighvat Sokk thanked Finn Thorkelson. He for his part had had a very good supper. He had enjoyed it. The earl was fortunate in that he had secured the services of the best chef in Iceland, a very smart fellow with the knives and spices and fires, Lifolf was the name. This Lifolf had given them for supper baked trout, then a lamb roasted on the spit. It had been a delicious meal. Of course they had brought plenty of ale with them. Speaking for himself, Sighvat had eaten and drunk so much that he was feeling very sleepy. He had maybe in fact drunk a bit too much. He hoped Finn Thorkelson and his friends wouldn't think it discourteous of him if he went back to the ship soon for a sleep. Also he had got his feet wet in the rockpools and he was afraid of catching another cold. As for mistakes, he knew nothing about any mistakes. He was a simple man of affairs who when it came to a question of duty did what he had to do. It was beginning to be very cold on the side of the hill now. The fire was only a few red embers. He would have to go to bed quite soon as there was bound to be a lot of work to do in the morning and he wanted to be quite fresh for that. He would just have one more jug of ale, then he would go back to the ship.

Hold Ragnarson said he hoped Sighvat Sokk and the others wouldn't go away just yet until this vexed question of the numerical mistake was settled and out of the way. It was very dark in the island, it must be after midnight. What was that plashing out in the bay, a seal? Never mind. It had been unfortunate that this mistake had come about, not to say disquieting. It had got their peace conference off to a bad start. In the old days such a mistake would have been called ominous. He himself wanted to believe, like his friend Finn Thorkelson, that there had been a misunderstanding as to the number of ships and men that each party was to bring to Egilsay. He remembered quite distinctly that they had all been definite at the preliminary meeting in the cathedral in Birsay as to the number of ships: two. He remembered in addition visiting Havard Gunison at Havard's farm just before Lent – they had had a very pleasant drink together in front of the fire – and Havard Gunison had said when they parted, 'Next time we meet, Hold, will be in Egilsay at Easter, when we go there with our two ships each and our twenty peace-makers.' 'Yes, Havard,' he had answered, 'and the dove fallen and furled between us.' (The Yule festivities, Hold said, had made him poetic – that always happened whenever he and Havard Gunison had a pot together.) Speaking about Havard Gunison, where was he? Hold didn't see him there tonight. But of course in this darkness you could hardly see a thing. Havard was one of Earl Hakon Paulson's principal negotiators: he ought to be present. There had in addition been a definite agreement as to the number of men in each party: twenty unarmed men, palm-bearers. It was beginning to get lighter along the shore, or perhaps it was that Hold's eyes were getting used to the darkness, but it seemed to him that there was a sharp gleam lying here and there among the heather. His friend Finn Thorkelson had said truly that mistakes were an everyday occurrence in life – he knew one mordant man in Shetland who held that life was one huge mistake (but let that pass) – and Finn had spoken about the kitchen girl killing three ducks instead of two. Three for two is a natural simple even touching mistake; one smiles to think of the girl and the angry cook; but to mix up such widely divergent numbers as two and eight argues what seemed to Hold to be a dark devilish interference in the straightforward dealings of men.

Sigurd Kalison asked the boy Flok to fill up his horn with ale, and perhaps he should carry some over to Sighvat Sokk too, if Sighvat wasn't asleep. All this talk had the effect of making him very sleepy. He was tired of talk. What he liked best after a good supper was a story and a few harp-songs. He said he was sorry, he didn't think there was enough ale in the barrel for Finn Thorkelson and Hold Ragnarson and their friends on the other side. He expected however that they had ale in their own ships. Of course you couldn't stow so many barrels of ale into two ships as into eight ships. It had been nothing but talk, talk, talk, in Orkney for more than a year now. He himself, personally speaking, was tired of it. They must surely all be sick of it by this time, even Hold Ragnarson. It had seemed as if the islands were inhabited by a tribe of fishwives. Now, thank God, the talking was at an end. The time for action had come. Finn Thorkelson and Hold Ragnarson must be very stupid if they didn't see that. At least, tomorrow the time for action would arrive for (he was sorry to say) here they were in the middle of another word-storm. This, thank God, would be the last word-storm. What must be done would be done in the morning. One swift clean stroke would solve everything. Finn Thorkelson in his opening speech had said something about a mistake, an error in accountancy, something about a clerk and a letter. He assured Finn Thorkelson that there had been no mistake. This was what had happened. The previous Thursday night they had all sat down together in Earl Hakon Paulson's Hall in Orphir to formulate some kind of an agenda for the business in Egilsay the following Monday: more words, words, words. Havard Gunison wanted this done, wanted that said, wanted an emphasis here and a modification there. He, Sigurd Kalison, had felt, sitting there at that table, a deep stir of revulsion. Would the palaver never end, either here in Egilsay or in kingdom come?

He had looked up and seen, beyond the anxious moving
mouths of Havard Gunison and John Svenson (they were
arguing about, of all things, the exact order of the disembarka-
tion of the ships once they reached Egilsay, as between Earl
Hakon Paulson's personnel and Earl Magnus Erlendson's personnel), he had seen – he repeated – the dark knotted brow of
Peter Tusk the merchant and how he leaned his head, a white
weariness, on his useless fist, and then he (Sigurd) had known
for certain that they were all sick to death of lawyers' talk and
priests' talk. It was at that moment that the number eight had
cropped up for the first time, he believed from the mouth of his
friend Sighvat Sokk. It had been an inspired stroke. The mouths
of Havard and John had faltered and fallen silent. The hitherto
bored faces had looked eagerly and gaily from one to another.
Then all the company had turned their minds to arithmetic,
with special reference to the numbers two and eight. In the
secret juxtaposition of these numbers, it had been agreed
(except by Hold Ragnarson's friend Havard Gunison who
had dissented and had decided at the last minute not to come
to Egilsay) – that in that way and by no other means peace
would come to Orkney. A number was exact and clear and
efficient; not like words, bits of fog and wool. So that was the
position, whether they liked it or not. Hold was quite right, it
was getting on for morning, there was a grayness in the east.
There was perhaps not much point in going back to the ships
now, when there would be so much to do after daybreak. He
wondered if the boy Flok was there, because if so, he wanted
Flok to bring him another mug of ale.

Finn Thorkelson said that Sigurd Kalison had answered their
doubts and fears quite adequately (though he had used a large
hoard of the words he despised so much in order to come to the
point). They knew now exactly where they stood. He would
now have to broach a matter of the utmost delicacy. He was not
addressing himself now to Sigurd Kalison or to Sighvat Sokk. It

was useless in any case talking to drunk men, or to men so stupid as not to know the difference between 'eight' and 'two'. It was indeed getting much lighter along the shore. He could distinguish men from rocks, and axe-blades from rockpools. The fire was all gray ash. There was a rose-petal in the eastern sky, low down. It seemed to him that the unquiet shadow walking about on the hill, back and fore, was a certain honest upright august person in the councils of Orkney. At this moment that restless shadow was the most powerful man in the north. Finn Thorkelson went on to say that he was going to address himself now not to drunkards or liars but to the high-born person he had already referred to. (It was growing brighter every minute, he could see a flash of gold on the arm of the gracious listening shadow.) Well then, there was in Egilsay, apart from themselves, at that very moment, awake or asleep, a person who was loved by all the people of the earldom. This man of whom he spoke was of course precious to the people like Finn Thorkelson and Hold Ragnarson and all the others who owed him allegiance, but he was well loved too by men who in a political sense considered themselves his enemies – for example Havard Gunison, who had considered it shameful, because of some brutish error in arithmetic, to come to Egilsay that day. He believed there was affection between the man he was addressing and the man he was speaking of, a bond of kinship, the half-envious half-admiring complementary smile of oppo-sites. In addition, the man was the friend of the people. Most important of all he strove always (though he was a sinner like other men), he prayed continually and with utter trust and with deep questionings to be the friend of God. Well then, this dear one had come to Egilsay the previous day in all faith and trust and innocence. He was still in the island. To be quite frank he (Finn Thorkelson) had urged him to leave as soon as the confusion between 'two' and 'eight' had been recognized for what it was; but he had replied smilingly that he intended to stay, in the interests of peace. Finn wished to know now what the outcome of their unequal negotiation here would be: the peace of the cornstalk or the peace of the tombstone.

The boy shouted down beside the ships that the sun was up! the sun was up! the rockpools were burning!

The man with the golden ring on his arm began by saying that he was pleased to see Finn Thorkelson and Hold Ragnarson, and he went on speaking; but he spoke in such a low troubled voice that Finn and Hold had to bend forward, two black intent ear-touching silhouettes against the risen sun, to catch his words; and even so the phrases he uttered were interspersed with broken uncertain silences, so that in the end all they could piece together with any certainty from the fragments was that he hoped there would indeed be some kind of peace patched up in Orkney sometime later that day.

After the mouth of the man with the golden circlet on his arm had guttered with a few last incoherencies and silences, Hold Ragnarson said that he was glad it was now daylight, because they could see one another's faces clearly. The truth could be gauged from a man's expression, the devious shifting mask with which time had covered the enduring skull, better than from veiled words. He had hoped that they would all have come to the peace-meeting with bodies fed and rested, and with washed hands, and with mouths chaste from the kiss of the crucifix, for it was a confrontation that called for exceptional forthrightness and patience. But here Finn Thorkelson and himself stood, cold, hungry, outnumbered eight to two, on a bare hillside, talking with drunkards and a man whose speech was all distracted and broken up. Well, it could not be helped. He and Finn Thorkelson had certain serious proposals to make, and he hoped they would be heard in a right spirit (though he doubted it after what they had seen and heard that night). They, however, as the accredited representatives of Earl Magnus Erlendson, were quite prepared, indeed anxious, to face up

to the reality of the situation as it affected Orkney and all the
dependent territories round about – Shetland, Caithness,
Strathnaver – and all the folk living therein, whether secular
or spiritual, farmer or trader, bairn or death-ganger; a people
(let it be said) that had suffered long and grievously from the
differences that had torn the earldom apart. They were quite
prepared, having looked at the matter coldly and realistically, to
recognize that the root of the trouble was as follows: there was
simply no room for two earls in Orkney – all that anger,
generation after generation, pent up in a few small green
islands! Orkney would be much the better of being governed
by one earl only. This, let it be understood, was not Earl
Magnus's own personal opinion. Magnus considered that since
he had been born the son of an earl, therefore it was God's will
that he should rule in Orkney after the death of his father; and
that somehow he and his cousin Earl Hakon Paulson could and
must blend their opposed wills in a single benign purpose: the
welfare of their people. When he (Hold) said there should be
one earl in Orkney, he did not necessarily mean Earl Magnus. It
had long been apparent to Earl Magnus Erlendson's friends and
admirers, though they loved him, that he, Magnus, was not, so
to speak, possessed of any special skill in government or statecraft; he was not a ruler by vocation but only through the
accidents of blood and inheritance; and this – they had to face it
squarely – did not necessarily make for the weal of the state. Earl
Magnus's councillors recognized also that Hakon Paulson –
grudgingly they had to acknowledge this – was a man dedicated
and devoted to the art of government. He had an obvious
hunger for it. It was a passion with him. There was no greater
pleasure than for a man like himself, Hold Ragnarson, to be told
in simple precise unequivocal terms what the earldom's policy
must be with regard to Norway, for example; or at what rate
foreign cargoes were to be taxed at the anchorages. The
merchants, though they grumbled, liked being told by an

authoritative voice what goods they were to import and export, and how (for example) they must get so much Irish silver into the islands before the winter set in. Speaking as a farmer he (Hold) said that he and his fellow farmers welcomed advice from a disinterested far-seeing higher authority as to what crops they should grow, and how there was in such and such a summer a surplus of swine in the hills, and how it was conceivable that a part of the bog between Harray and Firth could be drained and cultivated. People liked to have their own private greeds and ambitions tempered by a neutral wisdom that took into account the weal of all the folk and not merely the profit that might accrue to this or that speculator; and this invaluable function, he acknowledged, Hakon Paulson could perform for Orkney. When such a man wore, alone, the coat of state, then justice and freedom and prosperity and destiny were no longer words, they became the atmosphere that men breathed. Hold Ragnarson went on to say he thought it might be possible – he could not say for certain – to prevail upon Earl Magnus, once he recognized the truth of the situation – and in general he listened eagerly and sweetly to the advice of his friends, though there was a core of stubbornness in him also – it was just possible that Magnus Erlendson might offer to leave Orkney for good and all. Earl Magnus was as much at home in Scotland as in Orkney. He had of course cousins at the Scottish court – mutual kin to himself and Earl Hakon Paulson – and indeed being the kind of man he was he had friends all over the Lothians and Strathclyde and the English marches. In time, he might well come to realize that his earldom in the north had been a burden to him. Magnus would be free of course to go about on horseback from castle to hall to monastery. A right welcome guest he would be wherever he went. The mountains and seas of Gaeldom would lie between him and Orkney; and of course if he agreed that day to such an outcome, Earl Magnus would have to promise in addition never to return to Orkney.

So, in such sweet and agreeable exile, Magnus Erlendson would live out his life, until such time as the silver cord was loosed, and the golden bowl broken, and the pitcher broken at the fountain. Of course, Hold Ragnarson said, he had no doubt that Earl Hakon would agree to his cousin retaining, in a purely honorary way, his title of 'earl'.

Sighvat Sokk said that in his opinion Hold Ragnarson spoke too much. He said Hold Ragnarson was suffering from a mouth-flux. He told the boy Flok to fill him another jug of ale. He had caught a bad cold through being out in the open all night. He ought to have been keeping himself warm at Lifolf's fire. Now that he looked he could see that Lifolf's fire was nearly out in the cave-mouth. Lifolf would have to be blowing it up soon to cook their breakfast . . . What would Magnus Erlendson be doing just then, could the gentlemen from the two ships tell him? Splurging in holy water in the kirk, to drive the seven deadly sins away from him – that most likely was what the poor creature was doing. It was time Lifolf was attending to the fire. He was very hungry for his breakfast. He wondered what Lifolf would be cooking for breakfast. Lifolf in his opinion was the best cook in Orkney, maybe in all Scandinavia if it came to that. What exceptionally good ale! He said that Hold Ragnarson spoke such shit it made him (Sighvat) so he didn't know whether to laugh or be sorry for Hold. If that boy didn't come soon with more ale he would kick his arse black and blue. Earl Hakon Paulson must not listen to all that smooth talk. They had come to Egilsay to do a job. The men from the eight ships knew exactly what must be done, and do it they most certainly would before they left the island later that day.

Earl Hakon Paulson (for in the full light of morning it was certain now that he was the man with the gold arm-ring) said that he was sorry he had not replied very coherently to the earlier remarks of Finn Thorkelson and Hold Ragnarson. He had not slept much these last three nights, in fact ever since the

number had been substituted for the word so suddenly in his
hall at Orphir; so there was a certain confusion in his mind. He
had considered it a matter of the dignity of the occasion not to
further steep his senses in drink, like some of the others who
had come with him to Egilsay the previous night; he hoped Finn
and Hold would excuse them; they would have gray ashen
mouths before sunset. He thanked Hold Ragnarson for the
gracious and generous words he had spoken concerning himself
and his ability in matters of statecraft. He had listened with the
greatest interest to Hold Ragnarson's estimate of the political
situation here in Orkney, with particular reference to the evil of
double rule under the suzerainty of Norway; and he could not
but agree with almost everything that Hold had said. With
regard however to the proposed voluntary exile of Magnus in
Scotland, there were certain difficulties. Both Finn and Hold
knew quite well that if this solution was put into effect Magnus
Erlendson, for all his innocence – indeed, because of his gentle
and guileless nature – would be used as a pawn by certain
potentates and magnates in Scotland in order to interfere, again
and again, in the affairs of Orkney. This had happened before.
Finn and Hold knew quite well that Magnus Erlendson had
come north out of Scotland seven years before, when he
(Hakon) was sole ruler of Orkney, and governing – he must
say this blushing, but it was generally regarded as true – with
some success and a certain amount of vision. Into that secure
scene – corn in the barns, animals grazing in peace in the fields
– Magnus had intruded, claiming his half of the earldom. He,
Hakon against his better judgement, had consented to that. This
was a matter of history. From that day the situation had
deteriorated in Orkney. He dared not risk such a thing happening again. Magnus would be no simple exile. His face would be
turned again and again northwards. The sword would be thrust
into his hand. Wax and signet would be put to papers he knew
nothing about. The solution that Hold Ragnarson had

propounded seemed attractive, but it was just not practical. There must be some other way.

A man shouted from the caves at the other side of the island.

Finn Thorkelson and Hold Ragnarson whispered together: a light and a dark intertwining sibilance in the silver air of morning.

A man called from the direction of the church: another answered. There were shouts all along the shore.

Finn Thorkelson said that he would like to offer a solution that would, he felt sure, be acceptable to Earl Hakon Paulson. It was this: Magnus Erlendson would embrace the religious life. He would become a monk, preferably far away, in Normandy or in Ireland. (That could easily be arranged. Every abbot in Europe would offer him a cell, for he would bring a huge endowment into whatever monastery was chosen.) Then there would be no such person as Earl Magnus Erlendson any more; he would disappear out of the world; his very name would be stripped from him; he would go with crossed hands in answer to the matin-bell, a simple brother among a hundred brothers; and nobody in all that monastery would know who Brother Anselm was, the one whose hands were clumsy with the plough. It would be, as far as the earldom of Orkney was concerned, as though Magnus was dead; for having taken his vow in perpetuity – as he would of course have to do – he would never set foot in all time coming outside the cloister. The severer and straiter the rule of the order to which Magnus would be sent – one, for example, which required perpetual silence – the better it would be, and furthermore it would be no hardship to Magnus himself, for he had long felt the attraction of such a life. Finn went on to say that he had once heard a terrible story; he did not know if it was true; but at all events he would recount it to Earl Hakon. It was this: a king of Denmark a hundred years before had captured one of his subjects, a count or a duke, of whom secretly he had long been envious and afraid. The king came upon this young nobleman by chance, when he was out hunting. The duke greeted the king fairly; but before he had time to understand what was happening, or to say farewell to his wife or to kiss his children, or to give orders about the work of his estate, he was gathered among the horsemen, and hoisted up and pinioned and hooded, and brought down to a castle on the loneliest part of the coast. Down and around and still down the warders led him, with torches, into a pit of darkness, and there, among the rats and the mildew, they chained him to a wall. The torches were put out. It is said that he lived there for many years. It is said that his eyes grew accustomed to the perpetual blackness; and so they put his eyes out in order to deny him even the comfort of glimmers and shadows . . . Finn said that he did not wish by any means to draw a hard parallel between the king/duke situation and the Hakon/Magnus situation (that would be to impute to Earl Hakon a ferocity that was no part of his nature), but to all intents and purposes Magnus, if he were to be immured in a monastery, would constitute as little a threat to Earl Hakon as the prisoner in his chains and his double darkness. One could imagine the desolate cursings of that unfortunate young duke against his tormentors, day after day, month after month, year after year, until in the end he resigned himself to a silent seething hatred. Brother Anselm's cell, on the other hand, would brim with perpetual prayer and beseechment on behalf of Earl Hakon and the people of Orkney; and great benefit would undoubtedly fall on the islands because of this hidden one who was interceding with God on their behalf. Finn Thorkelson said that what he envisaged (subject of course to Earl Hakon's final decision in the matter) was this: Earl Magnus, on freely relinquishing his earldom in the north, would do a thing it had always been in his mind to do, namely, make the holy voyage to Jerusalem and Rome. Then, on his return, the ship with the cross sewn in red on its sail would anchor in, for example, Dublin. A troop of horsemen would be waiting there. They would take the pilgrim westward on the last stage of his journey. They would leave the rivers and green fields after a time and come to a place where the western sea moved among rocks. An earl would bow under the round arch that was there; a novice would be received by the dove-like hands on the other side . . .

Lifolf the cook told two paupers who were lingering beside his fire that they'd better clear off. The gentry would be coming down to the cave for their breakfast any time now. They wouldn't be wanting tramps hanging around when they were eating. Well, if they were to come back later, round about noon, say, there might be a few scraps left – there was generally a sup left in the bottom of a flask, a bone with a rag of meat on it. Would they mind getting out of the way now till he put the chops and sirloins on the grill? There were dogs, wolf hounds, very fierce, on the ship, he warned them of that.

The boy called to the seals out in the bay.

Earl Hakon Paulson said that he was considering Finn Thorkelson's proposal closely. It seemed to him, on the face of it, to be a possible solution. He would have to discuss it with his councillors, of course. The longer he thought about it the more practical, indeed attractive, it seemed. Of course a great number of loose ends would have to be tied up. He congratulated Finn and Hold for having thought up such an acute solution. He wasn't of course an entirely free agent in this, others would have to be consulted, it would have in a sense to be the free decision of all the people of Orkney, as their opinions and feelings in the matter were reflected through the minds of the councillors on both sides. But it seemed to him, personally speaking, to be a first-rate idea. He didn't mind telling Finn and Hold that he and his men had come to Egilsay with an altogether different solution, the operation of which would have been sudden, violent, and simple. He had not liked it at all. It was not that he shrank from death. He had seen plenty of

death in his time, as Finn and Hold well knew, in Lewis and
Wales and Jutland: but honourable death in the sun – gules on
forehead and breast and groin, the generous interchange of the
gifts of heroes, ritual harp and axefall – all caught up, once the
fury was over, into the gaiety of a tapestry or a saga. He himself
had always hoped, perhaps vainly, that after he was howe-laid
there might be some saga that contained a sentence or even a
phrase about himself: 'Hakon Paulson was ever a generous and
brave and loyal warrior . . .' In that way a man lives on, a
fragrant ghost among the generations. But what would the saga-
man say about a furtive cold callous murder (that was how it
would be seen, no matter from what root of necessity and
realism the act had sprung)? His name would be bitterness and
winter on the tongues of men always. But now by a stroke of
inspiration Finn and Hold had saved him from that shame and
infamy. He could never thank Finn and Hold enough. He was
now quite convinced, in the full light of morning, that it was a
perfect solution, so obviously correct that he would not even
have to consult his advisers about it. They must see at once, like
him, the beauty and simplicity of it. All would be well. Magnus
would enter his monastery in the west. They would arrange it
between them down to the last detail before sunset. A ship could
be despatched to Galway on Friday.

Sigurd Kalison said they would see about that.

Earl Hakon Paulson said that now what he was longing for
was to greet Earl Magnus. Two mouths, a single kiss of peace.
Then Magnus after a few days would depart into his blessed
silence, and he himself would take up once more the duties of
state-craft which, if a man performs them well, makes him
worthy of a few favourable words in a saga. Meantime, where
was Magnus?

Sighvat Sokk asked Earl Hakon Paulson if he seriously
intended changing horses in mid-torrent? They had come to
Egilsay to do a certain necessary thing; in fact to work out

another piece of arithmetic, the simplest problem of all, the subtraction of one from two. They who wore the red coats were all quite determined about that, let Hakon Paulson indulge in whatever daydreams he liked. He would not really have thought, had he not heard it with his own ears, that Hakon Paulson could ever have been so credulous. They were not going to go back now on a solemn sworn oath. Before sunset there would be only one earl in Orkney. It was a matter of no importance to Sighvat Sokk what earl remained alive, Hakon or Magnus. But the decision lay with Hakon.

Earl Hakon Paulson said nothing.

Sigurd Kalison said that he agreed with every word that Sighvat Sokk had said. He could not have put it better himself.

Earl Hakon Paulson said that in view of the speeches that had just been made little remained for him to do but to present his axe to one or other of the gentlemen present. Some of them, he could see at once, were in no shape to wield the axe with the skill and delicacy that would be necessary. He observed that Sigurd Kalison's hands were shaking violently. He saw how Sighvat Sokk had turned away and how his chest was shuddering with spasm after spasm of asthma. What must be done now would be a kind of ritual, and so he was going to give his axe into the keeping of Ofeig Arnison. For Ofeig, by the nature of his calling, all life was a ritual, a sequence of heraldic stations. Ofeig would make of the axefall a pure cold act.

Ofeig Arnison (he was the pivot about whom the battles of Orkney had long revolved, the standard bearer, the crest of victory above the tumults, keeper of the woven magical talisman of war) said that in his opinion what must be done must be done, certainly. He differed however from Earl Hakon Paulson as to the quality of the act. It would be a filthy thing for any man to have to do – to kill a quiet man quietly, away from the trumpets and the hooves and the wild joy of battle. Merely to think of it struck a chill into his heart. He thanked Earl Hakon for his consideration but he preferred his own axe with the blunt edge and runes cut along the heft which of course he never used, even in battle, for the inviolability of his office was guarded by a hedge of axes.

Earl Hakon Paulson said nothing.

Hold Ragnarson said that it was a poor earl that couldn't impose his will on a hillside of drunkards. It was still not too late for a certain man to put upon a black drunken blood-splashed dance the stillness of the dove. The arm of the man he referred to was an intolerable blaze now in the noon sun.

Finn Thorkelson told Hold Ragnarson that he was wasting his breath.

Earl Hakon Paulson said he saw now that what was needed was a butcher, an ordinary tradesman who chopped meat and bones with a certain practised skill. It so happened that there was a butcher in Egilsay that day, or rather a tradesman who was both a cook and a butcher. Lifolf slaughtered the beasts and he also put them on the grill, and he was very good at his job, as all present could testify. They had eaten a good dinner last night – though they were all a bit gray about the mouth this morning. He doubted for example, whether Sigurd Kalison and Sighvat Sokk would be able to face the meal they had ordered. He told the boy Flok to tell Lifolf the butcher that he (Earl Hakon Paulson) wished him to come at once to the stone on the hillside.

One element of sacrifice is that the tribe, represented by a set-apart secret one, takes a certain measure from the tribe's hoard – something essential to the life and well-being of the tribe, a black passionate bull, say – and offers it back again to the mysterious source that gave it. It seemed to even the most primitive people that they and the animals that yielded them food and clothing had not come together by blind accident, but were parts of a three-fold relationship: as god-man-animal, as provider-hungerer-food. The god was to the herdsman as the herdsman was to the beast, yet all three were bound together in the potent mysterious wheel of being. That their cattle and sheep did not seem to be aware of the god was a part of the mystery; but in fact they acknowledged the god, in brutish simplicity and patience, by simply existing.

The animals honoured the god especially with their broken flesh and spilled blood. I do not speak of the shambles and the work of the butcher; I speak of priests, a solemn sacred ritual, lustrations, sacrifice. The kneeling beast, the cloven skull, the scarlet axe, the torrent of blood gurgling into the earth at the time of the new sun, the hushed circle of elders.

The god seems sometimes to be arbitrary and fickle – in that, for example, he deals out drought and famine one year, and teeming pastures the next. But this is because his nature is incomprehensible to men, he exists in pure serenity conversing with other gods, his great ox-eye sees not only this present generation but the whole life of the tribe from its beginning to its end. What the people take for arbitrariness is divine wisdom, omniscience.

In fact, in the god-man-animal relationship, it is only man who is the wayward unstable partner. His hands have done things that he knows to be wrong. His mouth has uttered filth. His feet have led him into dark places. He has dishonoured his secret members with adultery or time-wasting fantasies. He has not put food into his father's withered mouth. Or perhaps the whole tribe in a surge of madness has bowed to a stone in the desert at sunset. But still the tribe and the god are one (though the doings of men stink in the nostrils of the god sometimes); they are bound together; and out of this situation arises another mystery still – the god somehow depends on the tribe and the animals for his own awesome existence.

So a tribe of herdsmen and fishers lived, in piety and brutishness, in the islands between the two great seas.

Each spring the elders brought out a bull or a ram to the stone on the moor – not any old beast with withered loins, but a randy bright-hoofed yearling – and they offered him to the god.

The rain comes. Men stand about the foothills with shining upturned faces. A young man and a young woman look at each other secretly and shyly. In the dark of the evening more rain falls. The old men sit outside the huts drunk, the bowl goes from mouth to mouth. The animals go knee-deep in the new grass – drought or plenitude, it seems to be all one to them, they are utterly self-contained. The god is lost behind the thunder-clouds and rainbows. Yet all are caught up in the surge of fruitfulness. God and tribe and animals dance together.

An essential of the sacrifice is that the action, though see-mingly bloody, should contain nothing of rage or terror. Cleanly the knife passes into the throat; the blood comes out in one pure red torrent; and so the exhausted winter earth is nourished. A further mystery is enacted now. When the hands of the priest and the elders dabble in the blood the whole tribe is ritually washed clean of its blemishes and of the offences which in the eyes of the god it has committed. The earth flames with blood – the sin is consumed – the heart is purified.

It is on certain days, and at certain times of the year, the solstices of light and dark and the equinoxes for example, that the god and the tribe and the animals come together in especial intimacy. At the moment of sacrifice on the wine-dark moor, inside the stone circle, the god and the tribe and the slain beast share in each other's life. A man eats a dripping sliver of ox imbued with divinity and thereby he (the wayward one) takes into himself both the sweet-ness and wisdom of the god (in so far as his being can bear such intensities) and also a draught of the dark primitive power of the earth. The whole tribe kneels with reddened mouths. It knows then what it truly is, a dedicated people, one with the stars and sun and with the fruitful fires at the centre of the earth.

*   *   *

I have spoken of sacrifice as it might have been celebrated at Brodgar in Orkney, by a simple pastoral tribe, four thousand years before the time of Magnus and Hakon and Lifolf.

There were other more terrible altar-stones, in cities east and west, that these herdsmen and fishers knew nothing of. In some of those far-off temples, god-intoxicated, smitten with excess light, ruled by a mathematician-priest who divided the sun with exquisite precision into a thousand segments of fate and fertility and doom, it seemed unworthy to offer to the god the guts of an animal. Instead a young man was drawn one morning from the company of the laughing hunters, and led garlanded out of the woods, and set apart, cherished, cosseted all winter in a white place by white adoring hands.

The chosen one was always beautiful; but much anxious discreet inquiry went on in the stews and the dark places of the city as to his chastity, and if it was found out that he had so much as bared a girl's shoulder in the candle-light to cool the ardour of his mouth he was let go once more among the hounds and the flagons and the chessmen. The temple girls – his purity having been proved beyond a doubt – called him 'the beautiful one'. They called him 'the sweet prince' (though he might be no more than the son of a rope-maker). They called him 'lord'. Perhaps he grew tired towards the end of winter of his diet of figs and goldfish; and the minute examination of his excreta by the diviners; and the endless lulling of flutes. They called him 'the chosen one'. They called him 'loved of the gods'. Then one morning, between dark and light, the guardians of the temple led the young man, naked now, the three hundred and sixty-five steps up to a stone on the side of the mountain. An intolerable point of light touched the horizon. Two mathematician-priests laid the victim along the stone. The sun, thrusting slowly up, reddened ten thousand faces in the square below. When the sun was exactly bisected by the horizon the king-priest flashed his knife over the stone. He tore the heart out by the roots. He held up the palpitating life of 'the beautiful one' to the sun.

And the sun-god accepted it. He feasted on the beauty and purity that the city had so carefully cloistered and nourished for the god's delight.

Therefore the sun gave prosperity to the city. Gold came in cartfuls out of the mines to the workshops of the goldsmiths; from there to the temples and to the palaces and to the boudoirs of the courtesans. And therefore too the sun averted from the city the recurrent dream that troubled the seers; namely that a bronze-breasted blue-eyed tribe would come out of the east in ships and take their inheritance from them.

Because that city had gazed too ardently into the eye of the sun, and had taken to itself more of the god's substance than its being could bear, and because it had despised and disowned the deep earth-sources from which its own animal blood was drawn, at last, many years after the dream, an exact time-cycle the subtlety of which eluded the highly-skilled mathematician-priests (yet it must have existed in the mind of the god in complete precision and beauty) – then, on the stroke of the gong, the fair-haired destroyers came out of the east in their ships.

A festival, a shared meal, a song of praise, a death and a renewal, a dancing together: every sacrifice has these elements in it. Who first tore long wounds in the earth and sowed in it the seeds of wild corn nobody knows, but it was one of the great discoveries. The winter after that the women laid on the tables circles of bread beside the baked fish and the sirloin, and a new taste entered the world: an earth food that was altogether lighter and pleasanter in the mouth and the stomach, and was even more nourishing. We know the name of the first priest who offered bread and wine on the altar instead of a slain beast: Melchisedec the Israelite. This was a thrilling moment in the spiritual history of mankind. Nor was the pattern altered in the concert of god and man and the animals: for the earth had to be wounded in order to contain the seed, and the ripening corn drew its sustenance from the same deep sources that nourished the animals. Moreover it was a clean sacrifice, not the deluge of blood over the altar and the desperate flailing of hooves. Instead bread shone on the tongues of the worshippers, and the redness that stained the brim of the chalice was wine. Also the god of the tribe, it seemed, was well pleased with the silence and imma-culateness of the new offering made by Melchisedec. Men uttered new words to one another – 'pity', 'mercy', 'love', 'patience', 'peace' – as if this new food in some sense quickened their minds and hearts. The faces of those who sat apart and meditated shone with a new wisdom. But the old priests still selected the best yearling ram for sacrifice according to the ancient rites, and when there was a worm in the ear of corn, in desperation they dragged into the temple many young rams; then there was a score of reeking throats about the altar-stone, a holocaust.

But the god himself remained an enigma, a remote unseen august mystery, who on a rare occasion might thunder from the mountains or set on the prophet's mouth a burning coal.

What if the god were to choose to play a more active part than ever before in the three-fold relationship? There was nothing to prevent him if he so chose. The god had a deep passionate concern for his tribe – the scholars could trace his workings and salutary interventions all through the sacred books of their history.

The beast was dragged to the altar-stone. Bread and wine were carried to the altar-stone. A young man in certain fanatical cities went with songs and waving branches to the altar-stone. What – the daring of Melchisedec the priest was nothing at all to the stricken eye and halting tongue of the prophet who first announced it – what if the god himself were to come to the altar-stone, himself the deity and the priest and the victim?

The tribe must have fallen into a deep dark pit to require such unique assistance.

Yet to bring this about a man and a woman and a hidden one stood one night at an innkeeper's door in a village. And in the fulness of time the same hidden one endured gladly the fourteen stations of his death-going.

That was the one only central sacrifice of history. *I am the bread of life.* All previous rituals had been a foreshadowing of this; all subsequent rituals a re-enactment. The fires at the centre of the earth, the sun above, all divine essences and ecstacies, come to this silence at last – a circle of bread and a cup of wine on an altar.

Out of earth darkness men set the bread on their everyday tables. It is the seal and substance of all their work; their very nature is kneaded into the substance of the bread; it is, in an ultimate sense, their life. They bring a tithe of this earth-gold to the holy table. At the moment of consecration, the bread – that is to say, man and his work, his pains, his joys and his hopes – is utterly suffused and irradiated with the divine. *Hic est enim corpus meum.*

At certain times and in certain circumstances men still crave spectacular sacrifice. When there is trouble in the dockyards and there is no sound from the weaver's shed; when theologians brood over the meaning of such words as 'justification' and 'penance' beside dribbling waxflames; when the frontier tower becomes a strewment of stones; when black horsemen and red horsemen ride through the hills and the heavy heraldic coat is riven; when the deep sources are seemingly hopelessly polluted – then bread and wine seem to certain men to be too mild a sacrifice. They root about everywhere for a victim and a scapegoat to stand between the tribe and the anger of inexorable Fate.

So Magnus Erlendson, when he came up from the shore that Easter Monday, towards noon, to the stone in the centre of the island, saw against the sun eleven men and a boy and a man with an axe in his hand who was weeping.

I lived at that time in an old forester's hut just outside the compound. There were pine trees above and the ground sloped up steeply towards the mountain. Below were the lake and the village. Of course the cookhouse where I did my work was inside the compound. I was the chef in the administrative wing. There were half a dozen kitchen orderlies under me, including a Jewish boy called Rudi. We cooked for the camp staff. There was another cookhouse in the west section of the camp, for the prisoners. I had never seen it. I did not know any of the workers there, I suppose they were mostly prisoners themselves. I can't imagine what offal they dealt in, especially when food got very scarce in the third and fourth years of the war, the time I am speaking of.

I liked my work well enough. You know, they were all decent to me, except for one or two of the non-commissioned officers. The less said about them the better. I was left, outside my work, completely to my own devices. It was comfortable in the hut. I had this girl Lotte who used to come up from the village to see me at the weekend. She often brought up cheese and wine. Lotte had a guitar and we would sing beside the log fire. I suppose the authorities gave me these privileges because I was good at my work. I'm a qualified chef. I passed second out of forty at the catering school in the first year of the war, and I'm proud to say I worked for a whole winter as assistant chef in the Hotel Mozart in Munich just before I volunteered. I was under the great master-chef Svenski at the Hotel Mozart. Apart from the cooking, I obtained a second-class certificate as a butcher. Not a slaughterer in an abattoir, you understand, nothing like that – what we learned, under Herr Krull, was the different cuts of animal and the cooking potential of each. It is quite a science in itself. I mention this because it is part of the story I have to tell.

The time I'm speaking of was the fourth April of the war. We all knew that things weren't going so well in the east, and we had steeled ourselves for a long hard war. The previous winter there had been a huge extension to the camp. Half the forest was cut down to extend the compound. Russian and Polish labourers did this work. It was a cold winter and I heard later that many of them died in the snow on the mountain. The work was finished at last and then the prisoners began to arrive in droves. The little railway station in the village had never been so busy. New prisoners came every day by train from the cities. The journey must have been far from comfortable. They arrived in cattle trucks, men, women and children, thousands of them.

Of course it had nothing to do with me. I had plenty to think about reorganising the kitchens to feed the camp staff that also were increasing in number every week. I had to apply for new kitchen workers. It was a continual worry, because the rationing got much more severe that winter and spring. I didn't have much time to worry about things that were no concern of mine.

A new camp commandant came in January. I saw him arriving in a large black car. He was a tall erect thin-faced man with the rank of colonel. A small band played for him at the gate, trumpets and horns. He walked on past that music as though he never heard it. He had his quarters somewhere in the new administrative block.

My work was usually finished by six in the evening. I had two good under-cooks that I could depend on to see to the carving and serving up. It was always good to be back in my hut outside the compound. I had my books, a lot of Edgar Wallaces especially, and an old horn gramophone and a few records. It was good to get away from these alsatians prowling about in the yard. The air was clean and cold between the pines and the lake. The prevailing wind seemed to come between the mountains and it took all the sounds and smells of the camp away.

On several afternoons one week in March there was an unbearable stench all over the compound. It was horrible. It was something completely new. The stink seeped into the kitchen where we were working. It was a loathsome sweet indescribable smell of charred bones and excreta. The Jewish boy Rudi who was sweeping the floor the first time I experienced this smell said that it was the new ovens in operation, beyond the barbed wire.

It had nothing to do with me. The air was clean and cold around my hut. There was this wind always from the mountains, bringing the scent of pines. I could spend the evenings as I wished. At weekends Lotte came up with her guitar. I was happy enough.

Lotte said there were plenty of rumours in the village about the camp. They all knew that the people who were arriving in the cattle-trucks were Jews from the east. The villagers were furious about the stench from the camp. Two days that week a poisonous green cloud had hung over the village, in the frost. Herr Schmidt the grocer had wondered whether he ought to complain about it. I told Lotte, quite sharply, that the village should mind its own business. There was a war being fought. Everyone must expect to put up with a certain amount of unpleasantness.

Well, then, this particular Monday evening in April a couple of vagrants came to the door of my hut, a man and a woman. They could have been gipsies. God knows where they came from. They were a queer-looking couple. The woman was wearing a pair of glasses with thick lenses and they were tied round her head with string. It seemed to be mad and reckless on the part of people like that wandering in the vicinity of a camp – there was a sizeable number of their kind inside, mixed up with the Jews and the Poles. I found a piece of cheese in the cupboard for them. The man thanked me. They were as quick and cautious as foxes. They turned and made off in the snow in the direction of the village.

The gipsies could hardly have been out of sight when there came a sharp knock at the door. It was Corporal Jasyzk to say I was to report immediately to the camp commandant's office.

I was more than a bit apprehensive. I had no idea what the camp commandant wanted me for. Could it have been something to do with the gipsies? If it turned out that they were spies, or escaped prisoners, then it might well be that I would find myself in a bit of trouble. It was every citizen's duty to report suspicious circumstances at once. I remembered too my great-grandfather in Lübeck, Hans Rosenberg; there was this slight Jewish tincture in my veins. Had some insect of a clerk been boring through the city registers, far north on the edge of the Baltic? I went with Jasyzk through the compound and into the administrative block, then through a long corridor. A beautiful clerkess in uniform went from one door to another with a file under her arm. I had never been in this part of the camp before. We entered a lift. Jasyzk pressed the button. We emerged on to another corridor three floors up. We walked past doors with names and ranks stencilled on them in Gothic letters to a door at the end of the corridor that had a large swastika painted on it. My heart was knocking louder than Corporal Jasyzk's fist on the panel, I can tell you.

We were bidden to come in.

Inside were five officers, and a smell of drink. I knew one or two of the officers by sight. They were all fairly new to the camp. They stood and lounged here and there about the office. A young major was sitting on the desk, swinging one leg. The camp commandant stood looking through the window towards the lake and the village. His back was turned to the others. There was a half-empty brandy bottle on the desk, and a few sticky glasses here and there. The air of the office was a blue and gray drift of cigarette smoke.

'Have I the pleasure to address Herr Lifolf the camp butcher?' said the young major. I realized that he was quite drunk. You know how it is when drunk men speak – there is a slovenliness in their utterances and yet they place their words with great care like setting out dominoes on a board. Two of the other officers were very flushed in the face. They stood around with glasses in their hands. One wore a monocle. A balding gray-haired officer, a captain, gave me a slack wan smile. The camp commandant was the only one who did not have a glass in his hand. He continued to stare out of the window. I could see only his thin profile against the sky.

I told the young major that it was possible there was some mistake. I was principal chef of the administrative section of the camp. On the other hand, I had qualifications as a butcher too – I had learned the trade in the catering school of Leipzig under Herr Krull and had obtained a second-class certificate in the subject. But butchering was not my proper trade. Principally I was a cook, a chef.

'Herr Lifolf, you will have a drink with us,' said the major. He sloshed out brandy into a glass and pushed it along the desk towards me. The glass had been used already – it was all stickiness and mouth stains. A captain with a scar at his neck said in a thick voice, as though he had a bad cold, 'I think you will be suitable, Herr Lifolf. We have a job for you to do at nineteen hours precisely.'

I do not drink spirits, but I thought it best to go through the motions. I touched the brandy to my lips. I thought that this must be some kind of a party, for Easter or because it was somebody's birthday, and they wanted a special meal for later in the evening. It was a nuisance, after work hours, but it would have to be done if they wanted it. One does not dispute with one's superiors inside the barbed wire. I said I would do my best to give satisfaction. But I thought to myself, 'How on earth am I going to lay hands on salmon or venison at this time of night?'

'Well spoken, Herr Lifolf,' said the lieutenant with the monocle. 'It is simply a question of hanging a carcase. The

Magnus

worthy Herr Krull must have instructed you in the art of hanging carcases. Please to have a cigarette.'

So, they had shot a stag on the mountain. That was my next thought. They were celebrating the kill. They had sent for me to cut it up and salt it. 'Certainly,' I said. 'That will present no difficulties.' (It is in fact a filthy job.)

'Herr Lifolf,' said the young major, 'I begin to like you more and more. You answer like a true German, with promptness and precision and a willingness to carry out orders. I am sure that you are the man for the job, even though butchering is only your secondary trade. I note however that you have not drunk your brandy.'

I said that my instruments were in the cookhouse – if they could please arrange for the carcase to be brought around to that part of the camp.

'That will not be necessary,' said the bald-headed captain. 'We have suitable premises in the basement of the east wing. You do not know this, of course. It is known only to a few. In the cellar of a block in the east wing. You will find the place of interest, Herr Lifolf. It is fitted with exactly the hooks of your trade, in stainless steel.'

The officer with the monocle began to laugh. He was sitting in a wicker chair beside the fire. Some brandy spilled out of his glass. He laughed like a certain type of woman at a clever filthy joke. His kneecap was wet. His monocle fell out of his eye.

'Herr Lifolf,' said the major seriously, 'I do not think that still you are aware of the nature of the task which we are asking you to do. For any true German it would be a great honour. You do not require to be told that we are at war. Certain hostile states we are confronting honourably and bravely. We do not fear their soldiers. The enemy we fear is the enemy within our borders. Here in this camp we have a special task, to destroy such bacillae – Jews, gipsies, socialists. Herr Lifolf, I should be pleased if you drank your brandy. We proceed tonight to the elimination of one of those enemies. A man is to be executed. I will tell you about this condemned prisoner. For years he has spoken about such things as "the brotherhood of man", "the spirit of peace that ought to brood upon all the peoples of the world", "the universal kingdom of love". (I use some of his own hackneyed phrases.) Herr Lifolf, nothing softens a nation's will to victory more than such talk. The man was warned over and over. He was visited by the political police. He has been given every opportunity to leave the country. We did not wish to touch him too closely – he has a certain world fame. The man would not hold his tongue. Through the ruins of our cities he went with his poisonous olive-branch. We have proof that he sheltered Jews and spies in his church. He was arrested last winter. In January he was sentenced to death. We have received instructions from Berlin. Tonight the sentence will be carried out. It will be carried out in this camp. We wish to show this pure spirit, by means of the butcher's hook, that he is, after all, when all is said and done, an animal like other men.'

I said to the cold face at the window, 'Herr Commandant, I am sorry, I do not know what the major is talking about. I have never done such a thing. It is not in my nature. I ask you to relieve me of this duty. I am a chef, not an executioner. I am a butcher only in so far as I know how to cut up the carcases of animals. I do not know the man they are speaking about. It is inconceivable that I should do such a thing to another human being. Even though this man is an enemy of the state and deserves death, there must be an official executioner in the camp, one who has studied the craft and knows what must be done. Let him be sent for. I am not capable of such a thing. I am a man of peace. I was intending to play gramophone records when Corporal Jasyzk knocked at the door of my hut.'

The lieutenant with the monocle tittered again.

The clock on the desk stood at a quarter to seven.

It occurred to me that I had been drawn into a huge charade. They wanted to have an hour's fun before they sobered up.

'I beg pardon,' I said. 'It was of course only a joke of the officers to summon me here. I am always being told by my friends that I am lacking in a sense of humour. But it is more, I think, that I am slow in the uptake. I am, after all, Herr Commandant, just a tradesman who happens to have been directed to this camp by the military authorities. I have not had the advantages of these officers' education and culture.'

The face at the window glinted like an axe.

'Herr Lifolf,' said the young major, 'you have a fine flow of eloquence. You will exhaust yourself with words. I am afraid the decision has been made. The Herr Commandant has signed the order. The joke is about to be put into operation. It is a good joke too. See how Lieutenant-Colonel Sigurd is weak with laughter already. We will proceed to the execution shed at once. I would strongly advise you to drink your brandy.'

All the officers were on their feet now. The asthmatic captain began to cough in spasms in the gray hot air of the office. The lieutenant-colonel could not get the flame of his lighter to the tip of his cigarette; he threw the scorched soggy thing into the fire. One of the other officers staggered when he got to his feet. The office clock stood at five minutes to seven.

The office block circled round me. I was drawn, by stair and corridor and lift, deep down into the hidden heart of the camp. Somewhere here the indescribable stenches had their source. New faces came about me.

The room I stood in finally was a whitewashed cube. There was a single electric bulb in the ceiling. Into one wall about eight feet from the floor three steel butchers' hooks had been screwed. A short noose hung from the right-hand hook.

A sergeant said, 'Everything has been prepared, Herr butcher. The prisoner will stand on that stool. Your duty will simply be to put the noose about his throat. I will raise my hand. That will be the sign. You will then pull the stool away. It is simple.'

Masks entered in at the door, and among the masks one living face. I had seen that face before, though only in newspaper photographs and newsreels. He was the Lutheran pastor whose books were burned at the start of the war. There had been much talk of him when I was a young man. The things he said and did were reported everywhere. Then suddenly it was as if a great snow had fallen on him and buried him.

He stood in the centre of the floor reading out of a prayer book. His lips shifted silently in his vivid face. The sergeant set the stool under the noose. The butcher's hook flashed.

The man had a look of sleepy wonderment. 'In these times,' he said, 'a man must read his own funeral service.' He closed the prayer book. He kissed it. He smiled.

Captain Sighvat began to read the death sentence in a slurred staccato. 'We know all that,' the prisoner said. 'Let's get on with the fun.'. . . He spoke as though it were some kind of game at a party.

To me he said, 'You don't look like a hangman.'

He gave me his prayer-book then. At least he must have, for I found it in my pocket next morning.

I remember saying something to him. I can't for the life of me remember what I said, though I have the idea somehow that I had never spoken so earnestly and passionately to any living creature.

It's funny what things I do remember. The bald-headed asthmatic officer Captain Sighvat, for example. He was standing in a corner of the cell. His face was like a clown, pure white with splashes of red on the cheeks.

I can't remember all the business of the stool and the hook and the noose. I can't even remember the sergeant raising his hand.

Harvest

The old wife stumbled on after. She held a torn fistful of cloth, a coat tail. Bright foot by dark foot, on they went. Their two mouths smoked a little in the eager early air. The old wife stiffened. First a lark began, a small wing-flutter in the next field, then up, spilling a few sleepy notes, and up, and threw a skein of shimmering notes about the ridge of Cairston. The song flashed and fell. The old wife tilted her head. She stopped. The two feet in front of her clumped to a halt. Their boots were saturated with dew. Another lark sang, further off. The sun put a first cold beam on Jock's face. He pulled away. Mary stumbled on after. Bright foot, dark foot, bright foot, dark foot – even in the growing light the hindmost foot was dark.

– Where are you taking me? What's the hurry?

He did not answer immediately. A whole day was in front of them. There was small point in rousing churlishness. Bright foot, dark foot, bright foot. But at last he spoke.

– We're going to the Birsay kirk.

– Kirk? What are we going to a kirk for? There's nothing to eat in a kirk. Oh no, I'm going to no kirk. I can assure you of that. Kirk, indeed.

A faltering of feet. Then Jock dragging on again, vexed for the thousandth time that he had ever answered her. They smelt, suddenly, sea and seaweed and fish. Insane scolding of gulls between a boat and a pier. Dawn stained the water of Hamnavoe, for two eyes, with crimson and primrose and jet. Wing-thresh and barbarity of gulls over a heap of fish on a pier. The fishermen sliced the gray cowled heads off, flung them into the harbour, ripped the bellies open, flung guts into the harbour, swilled silver shape by silver shape in cold sklinters of sea, stowed the catch in neat rows in a fish box.

The old wife hustled the old man in the direction of the fish smell. Dark feet, bright feet. She pushed him. Her nostrils twitched. She heard the tearing of knives in haddocks' bellies, rhythmic and regular. She let Jock go. She stumbled, a dark foot, into the silver circle.

– Watch out!

A fisherman's alarmed shout. She knocked into the box. The box tilted. Fish slithered on fish. Angry shouts then. A fish-smelling fist had her by the shawl. She spoke, humble.

– Sir, I'm blind. I'm sorry. If you could spare me one fish-head. We have a long way to go. I know a place where I could get some oatmeal to stuff it with. My man here – it's a poor existence I have with him.

A hard moving shell was thrust into her hands. A crab. The claw clashed feebly at her wrist.

– Go on now, away with you. We're busy. Get the hell out of here. The pair of you.

Jock drawing her then out of the broken cursing circle of fishermen . . . away from the edge of the water . . . past the houses where women were shutting their doors (as ever) against the tinkers . . . Out once more among the safer fields, and smells of corn and grass and dung.

– One small crab. The mean buggers. I got a hook in my hand.

She stopped. Jock stopped. She licked a bead of blood from her finger. The crab made a small heave in her other hand.

– Don't snap your claw at me, hunchback.

She groped for the mouth of the sack that hung over Jock's shoulder. She dropped the crab into that darkness.

Bright foot by dark foot, trudging on, past a quacking splashing duckpond, past a cornfield, between a pasture and a cornfield, beside crofts that closed doors against their oncoming, going on, veering from a loud dog, trudging on, bright foot by dark foot, into the silence of hills.

– My poor feet. I can't go much further.

Jock took her by the arm and set her down in a dry ditch. The sun warmed their faces and hands. He eased off one of her boots. Her sole was hard as a stone, but for one fissure in the skin between the big toe and the limp cluster of four. The crack bled.

– That'll be all right. That's nothing. We're half-roads to the place.

– What place?

– The Birsay kirk.

She eased the boot on over the heel and over the ankle and clamped it to her leg with a piece of string. She put her face close to his. She spoke in a soft gentle voice.

– I'm going to no Birsay kirk. You can go to the Birsay kirk yourself if you want to.

They sat for a while in the sun. Jock chewed a stalk of grass. He gave Mary a suspicious look. He felt in the pocket of his coat, as if to make sure that something was there that ought to be there. The crab made small scratchings in the bottom of the sack. Jock turned. He took Mary by the arm and lifted her to her feet. She breathed at him.

– Say Birsay kirk again and I'll leave you. I'll bugger off. So help me God I will. See how you get on without me, mister.

Four boots beat slowly on the peat track that went between the hills. She gripped his coat tail. She smouldered behind him. She sang low with rage.

– Just leave me at the first ale-house door. There'll be a time to go to the Birsay kirk, ay, and the Birsay kirkyard too, when we're dead and rotten.

The dark interior hills of Stromness and Sandwick stood all about them. The hills moved slowly round them as if to make a

way for them. A passing crow put blackness in her ear. A hill
croft shut its door against them. Moors and knolls and peat-
ridges made a way for them and came together again behind
them. There, in the silence of hills, the old one heard a scratch
in the dust, a lost wing-flutter, a bewildered cluck. She stopped.
Jock stopped. He saw a white agitation in the ditch. A chicken
had strayed from the croft on the hill. Jock lengthened his
stride. His coat tautened. She nearly fell on her face in the
heather. He dragged her on.

– It's a white chicken. There's to be no thieving today. Please,
woman. We're pilgrims. We need clean hands and clean hearts
for the thing we're going to do.

Mary let go of his coat. She turned. She bent towards the
chicken noises. She spoke kindly. She coaxed. Her finger
beckoned. The chicken looked, dipped, jerked towards her.
She struck. A twist of hands. The chicken hung, a tempest of
white rags for half a minute; then gradually the flailings
guttered. Mary stroked a quiet wing.

– There, sweetness. There. You won't be feared of the dog
again. No, nor the hawk in the cloud either.

She opened the mouth of the sack and dropped the chicken
in beside the crab. Jock hoisted the sack higher on his shoulder.
He looked about him in every direction.

– You've made a small snowstorm in the ditch. We better get
away from here. I want to die on my back. God forgive our
thieving.

Bright foot by dark foot, they trudged northwards all morning. They said nothing. The hills stood behind them now. They
went between ripe oatfields. Noon threw short shadows in front
of them. Westwards the sea glutted itself in the caves of Yesnaby
and Marwick; and collapsed, wave after long curling crested
wave, on the beach of Skaill in white ruin; and sang further out
in many distant Atlantic voices. The song of the sea could be
heard everywhere in Hrossey island.

They passed a church. Through its open door Jock could see a priest at Mass. Jock stopped and dragged off his cap. The oncoming dark feet scuffed his ankles. The bright feet went on again. The land began to rise before them, a long gradual incline. The road wavered upwards between pasture and moor and cornpatch. To the left, the surf broke now on the weeded stony mere at Marwick. The crab died in the sack. The sun tilted over westward. Four feet whispered in the dust. They had not said a word to each other for two hours. The old woman's breath came shorter and harsher.

– Don't go so fast. What's your hurry? Stop till I get my breath.

A halt. Slow listening tilt of the dark face. A few bronze shadows moved across it from the heavy fertile wedge of Revay Hill that thrust itself into the surging blue and white of the sky. She harkened, darkly.

– What's the hill whispering about? Whisper, whisper, whisper. I never heard such gossip.

– The scythe in the barley. It's harvest. The crofters are all out.

– What crofters?

– Mans and Hild. They're cutting the high field. Their neighbours are helping them.

They sat down in the heather. Jock stretched out on his back. He was tired. He closed his eyes against the intense blue.

The old wife listened. The rasping of scythes diminished. The reapers had crossed the ridge. They were cutting the barley on the further hidden side. At the end of the next lane, or the one after that, they would all sit down and eat their supper among the stooks.

Mary harkened. She crouched. She left the heather. She went like the shadow of a kestrel across the stubble towards the smell of cheese and ale. She tracked the smell to a rock in the corner of the rig. She felt about the lichen-and-granite and lifted something heavy from the cold side of the rock and stowed the loot under her shawl. She crouched and listened. Corn-whisper, corn-fall, breathings of an idle dog. She circled back, crouching, and ran on, and crashed into a stook. She cursed quietly. She flowed round the stook and groped the last few yards to the shelter of the ditch. She lay down among wild cotton and a runnel of water. She could hear nothing for a while for her own lung-tumults and heart-strokes. Then, again, corn-whisper, corn-fall, corn-whisper. She laughed. She held up a flagon of ale to the sun. A cowardly familiar voice then from low in the heather.

– God forgive you, woman. More thieving to answer for.

She knew it was late afternoon by the slant and mellow fall of the light on her face and hands. She plucked an ear of barley from her shawl. She hugged the flagon to her heart and laid out her length of suffering bones in the heather beside her man. The sun lulled her. She struck a bee from her cheek. Jock began to snore. At sunset, at the Birsay shore, they would have a feast of boiled crab and roasted chicken, washed down with Revay ale . . . A harvest voice cut across her drowsiness, but it sounded remote as a dream.

– Mans, the flagon isn't here.

One had been sent on to lay out the meal.

Harvesters surged up the ridge. Six scythes flashed in a row. The barley fell in long whispering yellow waves. Scythes flashed. Barley fell, bronze scatters. The crunch and sighing of fallen barley stopped. A dog barked. Jock snored erratically. Feet thudded close by. The old one jerked awake. Heart-thuds, heart-thunders. She opened in terror her blank eyes. A hard voice above her spoke.

– So. The tinkers. The tinkers are looking after the ale for us. Get to your feet.

And Jock's voice.

– Sir, I'm sorry. Sir, this is our ale. We've carried this ale from the loch-side at Kirkness. A woman there gave us it.

– Get rope. Tor, get that piece of rope out of the barn. We must tie this lady and gentleman up.

– Sir, I'm a poor blind woman.

– You will be taken to the factor. The pair of you. What'll happen to you, that's up to the factor. Take the flagon back to the rock. The factor hanged a tinker in Swannay last weekend.

– Sir, for the love of God. Please.

– If you're lucky the factor might only ship you across the Pentland Firth, away from honest folk.

– We didn't know it was your ale, mister. I swear.

The harvesters jeered all about them.

She began to mouth and to mutter any random syllable that came into her head, any nonsense that they might take for an abracadabra and a curse upon their fields and wombs and hearth stones.

The harvesters laughed louder.

Jock's voice again, black and dangerous.

– Lay a finger on me, you bloody ignorant yokel, and I'll—

A thwack and a thwack and a thwack. The crofter had struck Jock across the face. Tor was back from the barn with the ropes. The ropes creaked. The harvesters sniggered. A hand gripped Mary by the shoulder. The long hides hung loose at her elbows, then her arm-bones were drawn together. She cried out. Jock mumbled through hurt lips among the rope knottings.

– It's more than likely the ropes will be round your necks before the sun goes down.

Sweet Jesus have mercy. Sweet son of Mary. Sweet Jesus.

A voice falling, mild and querying, through the shouts and the mockery and the yelpings of the dog.

– What's the matter, Mans? What's going on here at all?

– The tinks. They thieved our ale when we were cutting on the far side of the hill. I'm taking them to the factor.

– A flagon of ale? They took a flagon of ale. Well, they're thirsty, or they wouldn't have taken it. God, man, there's a hundred flagons of ale in the barn. Surely we can spare them one.

– They don't work. They're a nuisance to the whole countryside.

– They take what they need, no more. Mans, I'm asking you to remember something. Three winters ago we were as poor as them. In the year of the horsemen we were poorer. All that's changed now, thank God. Thank God and Earl Hakon. We have more barley than we can eat. There's plenty for the king and there's plenty for us and there's plenty for tinkers.

The old wife staggered about in the light after the ropes were off her arms.

– This time then, all right. But let me catch them at that game once more and I swear to God I'll have them cut to pieces with the scythes . . .

She blundered towards the smell of Jock. She seized him by his shaking arm. She rasped in his ear.

– For God's sake. Hurry. Away, out of here. Before the clodhoppers change their minds.

Heaviness thrust into the sack: a flagon, a round of gray bannock, cheese. The croft-woman's good smell in her nostrils. The old dark hand touched the bounty.

– Enough, Hild. You've given them enough. Don't encourage them.

– Remember this, man. We're only as rich as the poorest one among us.

The old woman took Jock by the shoulder. She thrust him forward. She dragged him away, bright foot and dark foot circling one another. For of course the fool must linger always to utter his gratitude.

– Thank you, lady.

The fool. Thanks to *them*, the earth workers, the enemies. Who hate the free wanderers under the sun. She dragged him away, dark foot stumbling on in front of bright foot, tugging him on by his rag of sleeve.

– That Hild is a good woman.

– Sour ale that nobody else would drink. That's what she gave us. A bannock hard as stone.

They passed the end of the field.

Behind them Mans was rallying the harvesters.

– We've wasted enough time with trash. Come on. The whole field must be cut before dark.

They stood on the highest ridge, two black figures against the flaming death of day. The wind shook their tatters.

– It's cold all of a sudden.

– The sun's down.

– Still, there's a good fire in Prem's. It's the thought of that that's kept my feet going all day, the fire and the ale and somebody talking sense for a change. There might be a fiddle.

Bright foot drew dark foot down towards the burnt-out mill. A gray cloud, huge and hard as a chunk of granite, was toppling over them out of the Atlantic. Rain would come out of it. They were too old for soaking. Ten years ago it didn't matter. They went on uncaring then through rain, sun, fog, snow, thunder. 'Brother rain,' they had said, 'sister snow, lord thunder.' (But 'brother rain' had turned sour on them seven springs before – he had put the knot in Jock's shoulder and the knife in Mary's haunch-bone.) All that fine family-of-the-weather had turned against them. Fog choked them nowadays. They dreaded the batterings of the wind in March.

– Where we going?

– The mill.

– I'm hungry.

– You can eat in the mill.

– What about you?

– I won't be eating today.

– What's come over the bloody man at all. He won't be eating.

Bright foot, in a rush and sklinter of water, swung dark foot over the mill-race.

They heard, clutching each other for a moment, a noise inside the blackened walls. What? A ewe – a strayed pig – the ghost of the burnt miller . . .

The first scatter of rain-drops hit them.

Jock peered into the darkness. It was a man. It was a man with one leg who flopped like a seal from stone to stone. It was one of the horsemen who had been left behind when the war ebbed from Orkney. The creature by the look of things had taken up residence in the mill.

A surge of rain went over the stonework. The stones shone and dripped. Mary's face – all but the eyes – glittered.

– It's all right, woman. Come on in. It's the one-legged horseman.

The creature cowered into a corner from the voices. He held a hand in front of his face. He peered through his fingers. When he saw that it was the tinkers he smiled. When he saw the half-filled sack he hopped towards them along the stone bench. He touched the bulk of the sack with delicate fingers. Then he began his door-to-door chant, uttered a dozen times a day, to housewives all over the north.

– I am a badly disabled soldier. I fought in the late wars in Orkney. I have been a soldier to trade all my life and I have fought in Spain, Turkey, Ireland, and the Baltic. In the late war in Orkney I was hired by Earl Hakon Paulson to fight on his side. This I did, bravely and honourably, for two years. In a battle in the hills of Firth a horse trampled me and my leg was broken. Later it was cut off at the knee by a bright sword. Long live Earl Hakon. I helped in his victory. But since the hour of my wound I have had to beg my bread. Peace was signed. My comrades left me. I must beg my bread till the day I die. Wherefore, pity, kind lady.

– Don't 'kind lady' me. You stink, mister. You're the lowest stinkingest scum in the world. You stink worse than a dung-hill.

– I'm hungry. I haven't eaten today.

Rain throbbed on the stonework outside.

– Give him a bit of bannock.

– Not a crumb. I'm glad he lost his leg. There'll be no more war dances for him. Scum. He'll think twice before he puts on a helmet again.

The old soldier began to weep. He had practised weeping for a long time. He could make himself cry real tears. Tears shone now in his dirty thistelly face.

Jock opened the mouth of the sack. He groped inside and brought out the crab.

Wash and surge of rain against the blackened wall. Drops sang and spattered through the rafters. Outside, the burn ran faster.

– Here, mister, take this.

The old woman's quick descending hand swept the crab out of Jock's fingers. She clutched it. She put it tightly under her shawl.

– Nothing for murderers. I'm not biding here. I couldn't lower myself to eat in the company of a murderer. I know who drowned Arn in his duck-pond in Firth. It was him. I don't forget a voice. Come on, man, the shower's past. We'll eat in some decent place.

Bright foot and dark foot together passed out under a lintel of shining drops. The west was the colour of clear honey with the sunken sun. The black cloud had moved away south. It was crumbling slowly still over Tenston and the loch. It would finally destroy itself over the scarred ridges of Hoy.

The old wife heard the earth drinking the rain. The air was pure after the rain. The sky was like a bell. She heard an otter at the mouth of the burn. She heard a spatter of cow dung hitting the grass, a mile away. She heard the fold and unfurl of a hawk's wing above the ridge. She heard night coming down, the bright-dark dewfall.

They moved on north. Bright foot. Dark foot.

Her hand had touched the thistly face of the one-legged murderer. She shuddered.

They passed the shuttered door of the smithy that smelt of burnt iron.

– War's a good thing for blacksmiths.

– Yes, and girls and gravediggers.

– I'm smelling the sea again.

– We're going down into the village.

– There's a touch like silver in the air. A shiver.

– The moon's out over the village. A thin naked thing, like a girl on the night before her wedding night.

– Ah.

– I've watched the moon a thousand times. Always changing, changing, like a woman. I've studied the moon well. First, this trembling bride. Then a bee-wife with a honey comb. A few nights more and she's a red-faced washer-woman – she swills linen in the burn, bright shirts. Then she's a widow with a small candle.

– Jock the poet.

– In the end she's nothing but an old hag, a poor blind crone among the ashes.

– So.

– Then the black boards nailed over her face.

Mary sighed. Their moon-talk had taken them past the sleeping farm-dogs and the lighted doors in Birsay village. Now the holy island blocked out a piece of the horizon – a steep black holm against the drained honey of day. Lights shone here and there on the island, from the Hall of Earl Hakon Paulson and, more sparsely, from the bishop's kirk and cloister. Jock saw, thankfully, that the tide had ebbed far out. It would be possible to cross over to the island.

Bright foot led dark foot down over salt-bitten grass to sifting yielding sand. They stood there with their boots half-buried.

Then they sat down on a rock. Jock took off his boots and set them under the rock. He took off Mary's boots. The blood had dried between her sticks of toe.

– Where are we now?

– Never mind. Take both hands to the tail of my coat. Watch yourself. We're in seaweed. We're on slippery stones.

Dark foot was clamped in sudden coldness. Dark lips shrieked.

– Ah!

– Don't yell like that. The holy brothers'll hear you. You put your foot in a pool, that's all. Come on.

– The sea's on the one side of us and the sea's on the other side of us. We'll be drownded.

Sea voices sounded to left and to right of them. Defeated sea voices. The sea had yielded the island to the land for twelve hours. The sea retreated still. The old wife heard the sound of sleepy kittiwakes in the crag. She heard the plash of a seal. She rounded her lips and whistled. Jock jerked her arm to silence. He was listening for the last of the compline hymns. Afterwards the kirk would be left in darkness and silence until just before dawn.

– Is there an ale-house the place we're going?

– No.

She screamed as though she had stumbled into a fire.

– For God's sake! This is a place of silence.

– I put my foot on a razor-fish. Are there any bits of toe on the rock? That slippery stuff's blood.

– It's seaweed. Take hold of my coat. Follow me. There's only one more pool . . . and a wet stone . . . and a few shells . . . and sand . . . and now we're on the island. Be quiet. The bishop doesn't like the kind of pilgrims he's getting lately.

Jock listened for a moment. Then he went on up the foreshore. She stumbled after. Their feet made a small clatter on the loose flat stones. He paused. She bumped into him. Their

feet slapped on the last of the stones, whispered through sand.
She rooted her feet in the sand. He dragged to a halt.

– I'm not going a step further till I know where we're going.

– I told you. To the Birsay kirk.

She screamed at him.

– I'm not going to any kirk!

– You must.

– I will not!

Echo after echo came back from the low crags. A cave
boomed. He put his hand over her mouth. He said, gentle
and low and pleading.

– Please, Mary.

She tore her wild mouth from his hand. She screamed like a
madwoman.

– No!

A light came on in the kitchen of the hall. A disturbed bird
wheeled out over a dark sleeve of water and returned, com-
plaining, to its crag-niche. A shadow moved in the cloister. The
old wife's head trembled with betrayal. They held each other,
silently. When she spoke again it was in a low voice. She spoke
out of hopelessness and weariness and hunger.

– I'm tired of the holy talk of them brothers every time they
put a bandage on my eyes. *O my poor afflicted daughter, bear
your cross with patience* . . . I don't want any more of that class
of talk. Oh no. I've had my bellyful of that palaver.

– Stay where you are, then. I won't be that long.

There was a crude stair of undressed stones from the beach
up the shallow cliff-face to the grass. Jock mounted the steps
easily by the nakedness of the bride-moon. His bare feet made
no noise over the grass. The island was utterly quiet. He stood in
front of the black hulk of the kirk. He paused, listened. The
brothers were breathing in this cell and that. He heard whispers
of Latin and the low clack of beads. The kirk was deserted. He
depressed the latch and opened the door into an immense

sweet-smelling cave. It was dark but for one small hard light at the side of the altar – a wound in the darkness, a rose petal carved out of ruby-stone – and, under a stone cross at the side of the kirk, a guttering candle weeping last gray tears.

He placed fingers in a stone hollow at the porch and crossed himself quickly with the holy water.

Then he bent a stiff right knee in the direction of the red light.

Images leapt at him from three walls of the church. And stood silently again against the walls. He quailed under the stone stares.

He went forward, tremulously, down the nave. There it was, set in the centre of the aisle, a square of new sandstone with a carved cross – the tomb he was looking for.

He knelt down beside it. He opened his mouth. The sound of his voice in the huge echoing hollow startled him. He began again, whispering.

– Noble one, I made a tin pail for you in Rackwick last night. I was taking it here. It was for you, a present. She sold it in a Hamnavoe pub for porter. Mary. She has a throat on her like a salt fish. Or more like a smouldering peat. Or more like a bit of the everlasting brimstone. Listen.

In the kirk could be heard only the muted sound of the sea, still ebbing.

– I'll tell you what I'm here about. I won't hide it from you any longer. As if you didn't know my errand already. It's not me, it's that old woman.

Jock felt in his coat pocket and brought out a hunk of tallow. He held it for a moment at the dying votive candle, till it took light. He dribbled hot grease on to the tomb and set his offering up, a reeky flame.

– Beeswax. I'm trying to mind on a prayer. Light for light, Magnus. Ask the Lord God to put a glimmer back in her skull.

The pleep of the old woman entered the kirk on a stir of night wind.

– How much longer do I have to bide out here in the cold!

– A small blink only, Magnus. I'm asking no more. She was as shining a lass as ever walked the roads. You must have seen her in her best days, many a time, going to the Dounby Fair with pans and laces, among the ponies and the fiddles and the tilting bottles. She could see in them days like a hawk through crystal.

Stone and silence. His knees and hands and mouth were beginning to be numb.

A sound of laughter entered the kirk – zany half-drunken hilarity.

– I've drunk the ale. It's good stuff. I feel I could dance.

Indeed there was a brief broken rhythm from below, a rise and fall of feet among the shore stones. The stones clattered again. The old woman was wandering about the shore.

Jock tried to close his ears to all but what passed inside the ragged tent of light made by his candle. The living man spoke to the dead man through a door of stone.

– I'm not blaming you for not listening to a tink.

Silence. He knelt in the cold heart of stone. He covered his face with his hands. His hands were two cold stones over his eyes.

– She's nothing now. A mouth on her like a warped purse. Two stones for eyes. That's what Mary's come to. Just an old blind sack of sins.

The latch rattled, cautiously. He tried to shut his ears to it. Whimpering sounded in the porch.

– Jock, it's midnight. A rat ran over me.

A throb of anger went through him. His intentions were running out like sand. Between the interference of the old one and the matin-singing brothers there was little time left.

– All right, then. Say nothing. I was travelling through Birsay anyway, for rags. I just came in out of the wind for a minute. It isn't beeswax at all, this candle, it's whale tallow.

Nothing. Silence. The coldness was in his bones now. There were no rewards either for any quick-witted trimming of sails. Here you must stand in the utter nakedness of truth.

– I'll tell you what I'll do. I won't steal or swear any more. Tell the Lord God that. Truth, Magnus. No lies from now on. Every morning and every night I'll say the ten Hail Marys.

He took his hands from his face. He opened his eyes. The kirk was lighter, as if a thread of gray had been stitched into the night's blackness.

A cry outside, somewhere between the Hall and the cloister, a cry that would rouse the dead.

– Jock!

She would batten on him and feast on him and disgrace him and drag him down till the day of her death. She had power, it seemed, to silence the saints. He marvelled at her. He reasoned, still on his knees, that she was the one who saw clearly what they were in relation to the truth. He was the fool and the dupe. How could he ever have thought for one moment that the courts of heaven, taken up with their endless *Gloria*, would ever interest themselves with a couple of sun-eaten vagrants?

– Well, well, say nothing. Maybe it's all for the best. Folk take more pity on a blind person, you get a lot more ha'pennies on the road. There's more to spend in the pub at the end of the day.

He got to his feet. Outside, it was full ebb. He could hear the last glut of sea on a rock . . . But the arched window in the east of the kirk was changing. In the loom of the window more gray threads had been stretched. Now, as he looked, a yellow thread wavered across.

He was going to get nothing out of the man in the new tomb. Not by begging, pleading, promising, threatening.

There was another, the Mother of God and the Mother of all men. He turned, humbly, to a tall gray statue near the altar. The face was in shadow still. He could see the hands held out, to take the new-born infant, or the transfixed man, or any of her children in any pain or joy whatsoever as they travel from birth to death.

– Our Lady of the Seven Sorrows . . .

The door to the right of the altar creaked open. Jock flowed behind a pillar. He was caught now like a rat in a trap. God forbid it was that old Colomb.

– Who's there?

It was the kind bishop – but the kind tongue had this morning a wintry edge to it. Jock said nothing. But the bishop had seen the shadow dodging into the massed shadows of the transept.

– I know you. What are you wanting here? I couldn't sleep all night for the screaming of that old woman down on the shore.

Jock emerged into gray light.

– Your Reverence, I was asking the saint to help us.

– The saint. What saint?

– Saint Magnus.

– There's no Saint Magnus. You're wasting your time, my man. That's only the tomb of the earl who was murdered in Egilsay. You might as well pray to a stone. I'm getting a bit tired of telling that to all the poor things that come here. They're beginning to come now from as far away as Iceland and St Kilda – hare-lip and scab and consumption. Ugh!

– I'm sorry, Your Reverence.

– Whether this dead man is a saint or not is not for us to say. He might be. The authorities haven't decided yet. A man isn't a saint because all the tramps and comic-singers of the day think he is. When Rome says he's a saint, that'll be time enough for me and you to ask for his help. Do you follow me?

– Yes, Your Reverence. Thank you.

Red and azure and black the pieces of glass in the east window defined themselves in the cold pre-dawn. The small flame of Jock's candle was lost now in ever-widening circles of brightness.

– Bless your faith, all the same. The brothers are coming in to sing a litany, so you'd better go now. You had no business to be on this island at all, do you know that? This is private property.

– No, Your Reverence. Thank you. I won't come again.

There was a new sound in the sea, as if a hand was straying over a harp. The tide had turned. The waters of Orkney began to waver towards the hidden bride-moon.

– The old woman seems to be quiet now. She's sleeping under the rock, I think. You can cook your breakfast. Then off with the pair of you.

– Yes, Your Reverence. Thank you. We'll do that.

– I'll remember you both in my Mass.

Jock bowed himself backwards out of the kirk. It was warmer outside than in, as if the earth remembered the sun of yesterday. He turned and stood against the assembling colours of dawn. Behind him the kirk began to praise God in his saints. The stonework thrummed with dark mellow monotony. The interior was a throng of candles, brown shadows moving, a flung gleam and fume. The voices went up and down.

– *Kyrie eleison. Christe eleison. Kyrie eleison.*

Jock found the old one flung out on a patch of sand, newly awake, her eyes fluttering like moths.

– Come on. We've got to get away from here. Hurry up, I said.

She cherished a black yawn.

The sea fell among the rocks guarding the island. The sentinel rocks stood in seethings of the gathering flood.

– We should get a bob or two for the candlesticks. Did you pinch the chalice too?

– Shut your face.

Inside the kirk the rhythm of the chant altered. Awe in face of the Trinity gave place to a more familiar supplication. The monks began to sing. The Litany of the Saints of the North.

– *Saint Olaf the King, pray for us.*

Nor had all his fasting of the day before done any good.

Hunger prowled about in his belly like a rat. Also his face had
turned sore and swollen where the farmer had struck him.

– Is that all you left, the chicken neck?

The sand around the cooking can and the fire-blackened still-
smoking stones was strewn with bones and bits of crab-shell. He
shook the flagon. It was empty.

The old one cringed away from him. She covered her face
with her forearm. The blow never fell.

– I tell you what went wrong. There was too much badness in
you. The saint couldn't do a thing.

– *Saint Ninian the traveller, pray for us.*

The sea surged in from both sides. The rocks stood up to
their throats in the surge. Stone shifted on stone.

– I slept for a while. The birds wakened me.

But before the birds wakened the old one, it seemed she had
had some kind of a queer dream. Jock half-heard what she said
as he swilled out pot and pan in a rockpool and shook bright
drops from them and held them out in the wind to dry. She
babbled on, more to keep his hunger and frustration from
breaking out in violence than to entertain him. The whole world
in this dream of hers was shrunk to a few folk in a winter field.
One and all the folk lamented how poor they were. A merchant
fat as a pig proclaimed his poverty – one of his twelve ships was
wrecked on Braga. A farmer came next, girning – a rat was in his
barn. Then a holy brother – 'Oh,' cries he, 'I'm betrothed to the
Lady Poverty.' But then the queerest thing of all happened. Who
stood in the field but the King of Norway himself, hung with
silks and diamonds, and beside him that old one-legged soldier
that lived in the mill. The king and the soldier had one bone
between them. They passed this bone from one to the other.
They gnawed on it like two wolves. There was a kirk in the
middle of the field. It was an immense kirk built of red stone.
She had never seen such a big kirk. In the door of this kirk – this
was queerer than queer – three men were standing. Jock the

tinker. The bishop. A man she didn't know, a man with a red
wound in his head . . .

– Shut your face. There's a busy morning in front of me, with
the fires and hammers. No use going to Westray except we have
a few cans to sell.

The sun rose.

The sun rose – the harvest sun – an immense vat of thick red
primeval clay, brimming with corn and ale for the bewintered
people of the world. An old woman on the shore has been
fashioned (like all mortals) from the same lovely clay; but now
she is a worn-out begging-bowl. That day, as every day, she
knew that the pagan sun would give her a bite and a sup. Vat
and begging-bowl tilted, touched, pledged. The sun was on her
hands. She rose. She was ready for the road.

– Put a handful of sea on the fire.

The sun rose higher, lamp of the world. By its light men come
and go. Even at midnight, even in midwinter, the sun lends a
little oil for lantern, candle, taper. The lamp of the old woman
on the shore has been out for a long time past. She knew better
than to offer that broken thing to the sun.

– Hurry man. The sea's throwing her arms about the place.

Into the hands of every unborn soul is put a lump of the original
clay, for him to mould vessels – a bowl and a lamp – the one to
sustain him, the other to lighten him through the twilight between
two darknesses, birth to death. He strengthens himself, this
Everyman, with mortal bread; he holds his lamp over rut and
flower and snow and stone, an uncertain flicker. It is a hard hungry
road he has to go. Now and then the honey of a hidden significance
is infused into his being. By the vessels that he has moulded to his
wants he calls this mystery of longing The-Immortal-Bread, The-
Unquenchable-Light . . . At death he leaves behind the worn lamp
and bowl, and (a peregrine spirit) seeks the table of the great
Harvester, where all is radiance and laughter and feasting.

And some there are – God have a pity on every soul born – that love their lamps and their bowls more than the source from which clay, corn, and kindling issue forever; and, their vessels failing at last by reason of age or chance, they set out dark into the last Darkness, a drift of deathless wailing hungers . . .

The sun rose higher, loom of endless light.

Inside the kirk a tallow stump reeked and sputtered and went out.

A light that has once shone is never quenched. Can a diamond wither?

Harder than precious stones are acts of pity and praise and charity. The saints hoard them against our coming. With these jewels are purchased meantime many a miracle and blessing for the afflicted ones of the earth. The old man on the shore got to his feet. A freshening wind threw the rising sea against the island. The smallest spume-drop is not lost – it is here, there, nowhere, everywhere, a frail blown cluster of salt bubbles; but also an emerald, an opal.

– Quick. I got spray on my throat.

Not the frailest thing in creation can ever be lost. A word, a smell, a flower, may be the hard rich symbol, recurring again and again in a man's life, by which we instantly recognise him. Spume on the psalter in a Welsh battle; the quenching in a rockpool of the fires of lust; a cascade of spray over a hand steering a ship to an island – a single sea-drop has wandered through a certain man's life, signing the supreme moments, a symbol and a leitmotif; as if the notes of his existence were to be purity and pain. Especially near the great moments salt water stung him – war, love, death (and of course birth also, for besides the pure water of baptism a little salt is touched to the tongue).

This man was now in two places at once. He was lying with a terrible wound in his face in the kirk near where the old man and the old woman were girding themselves for the road: Birsay, place of his beginning and end, birth and sepulchre.

Also he was pure essence in another intensity, a hoarder of the treasures of charity and prayer, a guardian.

This fragrant vivid ghost was everywhere and always, but especially he haunted the island of his childhood. That morning he had been summoned by a candle, a small pitiful earth-to-heaven cry; its flame quickly quenched, and seemingly futile.

The wind went through the Birsay corn in deep surges; it whipped crests from the Atlantic waves. The sea was coming in quickly, flushing out caves and crannies.

Saint Magnus the Martyr accepted the tallow flame. He touched it to immortality, a hard diamond. The radiance he reserved, to give back again where it was needed.

A wave broke on a rock near the two old wanderers and cascaded them with spray, or with a squandered treasury of opal-and-pearl-and-emerald (it depends how you look at it).

The sources of Light were troubled for a moment.

A glister of oil spilled into a quenched lamp. The old woman stiffened.

She screeched. She put her hands to her face.

– Ah-h-h-h! You struck me! You tore my face! . . .

– Be quiet. Nobody touched you.

– *Saint Tredwell, virgin, pray for us.*

Mary whimpered. And rubbed salt scurf from her eyes. And was quiet. And bent down. She plucked, tremulously, a flower from the grass. She knelt. She murmured names – daisy, seapink, thistle.

– Don't torment me any more. I've had enough of you for one day.

– *Saint Cormac the sailor, pray for us.*

The old one got to her feet. She turned her glimmering face this way and that. Her finger pointed at the incoming ocean, then wavered over in the direction of Revay Hill.

– A plover. A teeock.

Jock dropped his half-sucked chicken-bone into the sand.

– It's a lark, Mary.

– That's what I said, a lark. I know a lark when I see one . . .
What's this scarecrow in front of me?

– It's me you're looking at, Mary.

– So. You had black curly hair last time I saw you.

She plucked a white hair out of her own head and looked at it
and gave it to the wind.

– God keep me from pools. God keep me from stones that
shine in the rain . . . I'm supposed to be grateful, am I? Well,
I'm not. Can I get the dark years back again? There's one place I
do want to see though, more than any other place, and that's the
Birsay ale-house.

She bent over the grass till her face shone like a woman at a
milk-churn.

– Buttercups. That was a good name to give them.

She took her shining feet down towards the shrinking sea-
eaten shore.

– Hurry. The stones are awash.

Jock stood looking up at the murmurous church. He crossed
himself. His lips moved.

– All right then, I'll find my own way across.

The great red vat-and-lamp-and-loom was high in the east
now. Under the sun the crofters of Orkney brought out their
peaceful scythes for the second morning of harvest. There were
glitters and flashes all over Birsay.

– *Saint Columba of the islands, pray for us.*

Jock kicked out the fire. He shouted up at the kirk.

– *Saint Magnus the Martyr, pray for us* . . . Jock the tinker
said it before any of you.

He put the empty sack over his shoulder and turned and
moved off after the sea-washed feet of Mary.